EMBARGO

and Other Stories

EMBARGO

and Other Stories

THEODORE
DALRYMPLE

MIRABEAU PRESS

Published by Mirabeau Press

PO Box 4281

West Palm Beach, FL 33401

ISBN: 978-0-578-67453-7

First Edition

MIRABEAU

To the memory of
Clinton Thomas Conatser (1971 – 2018)

CONTENTS

EMBARGO

The embargo was a success: the people were starving and the country was in ruins.

Not that it had ever flourished, of course, not since the first successful slave revolt in history. Ever since then it had been a byword for political pathology, regarded by the rest of the world with changing proportions of amusement, horror and pity, but always with a real thread of contempt. What could be expected of such people but a long succession of disasters and bizarre dictators?

The latest coup by the country's toy army that deposed its supposedly-elected president (who sacrificed chickens in the presidential palace to decide policy, mainly which enemies to arrest) outraged the world, if by world was meant members of the General Assembly of the United Nations, many of whose member governments had come to power by coup. It was decided, with a rare demonstration of unanimity produced by threat and bribery, to isolate the country as if it were a carrier of typhoid who worked in a posh restaurant. From a date in the very near future, all communication with it was to cease, and no one would be able either to enter or leave it.

Long having been inclined to go against the current, in whichever direction it flowed, I resolved to take the last commercial flight to the country before the shutters came down on it, as it were. The prohibition of such flights and all other means of reaching the country was the final turn of the screw. It was an impulsive decision on my part, and yet, at the same time, one that I had long considered taking.

I was going through a fallow period – more than a quarter of a century ago, but it could have been yesterday, as far as my memory is concerned – when the world declared its embargo. At that time, I would sit at my desk in my study, wondering in desultory fashion what to do next. No inspiration came; but it so happened that opposite me on the wall at which I stared was a painting which I had bought on a previous visit to the soon-to-be-embargoed country. Apart from refugees and requests for foreign aid, naïve paintings had for a time been the country's principal export, at least until the vogue for them in more sophisticated places passed and was superseded by some other whim.

The painting in question was one that had never ceased to delight me: it did for me all that I could have asked of a painting that was not a masterpiece. It delighted my eye, stirred my memory, provoked nostalgia and even philosophical reflection. I never knew anyone who was not delighted by it: for it always raised a smile while at the same time occasioning an indefinable melancholy. Of course, if you knew the country and the history from which it emerged, the effect upon you was all the greater.

It was of a jungle scene: not a real jungle, but an idealised one, the kind of jungle in which it would be unendingly delightful to live. Here the trees were broad-leafed and succulent, offering shade to the weary and overheated. Their foliage was of cool, dark hues, and each of the trees bore juicy fruit of unknow varieties, all within reach of an upraised hand and ready for the plucking. In the background was a deep blue river, another perpetual source of refreshment. It was a kind of Eden, an imagined paradise.

In the centre of the picture, in a slight clearing, stood two large cats, one panther-dark, the other with a yellow pelt with perfectly round and regularly-spaced black spots. The irises of their eyes were green and stared straight out at you, but around their mouths a knowing smile seemed to play. They were friendly, these powerful animals, as if the fecundity of the landscape had abolished their need for predation. They, too, would eat the fruit of the trees, and therefore spill no blood.

The painting, therefore, was of a prelapsarian state, a utopia if you like, such as suffering men always dream of. But in this case, for a number of reasons, it was particularly poignant. The population of the country were descendants of forced exiles from Africa, brought as slaves to work on plantations, and since its experience and that of its forefathers had been almost uniformly of cruelty and the most naked exploitation, however patiently or nobly borne, it was not surprising that it now dreamt of the life and land from which its ancestors had been so violently torn as having been without blemish, a heaven-on-earth by comparison with what it now suffered. Men in torment always suppose that their life is in some sense unnatural, that were it not for wickedness, whether that of their enemies within or without, their existence would be perfect. But there was more to the painting than that.

The effortless luxuriance of the jungle in the picture contrasted painfully with the deeply-eroded bleakness of most of the country, the majority of whose land surface was now a dusty fawn-grey mountainous desert. When it rained, the desert became a sea of mud which often flowed in an avalanche down the slopes and gouged out gullies, so that the landscape resembled the skin of a very old person who had been for too much of his life out in the sun. And this was all the more distressing because the whole land had once been heavily forested: but now practically every tree had been cut to make charcoal, and even the sparsest vegetation could not survive. The desert was therefore man-made and everyone knew it; the perpetrators had been driven by necessity, which is more often the mother of short-sightedness than of invention. They had been forced by their own destructive activities into the noisome slums of the towns and cities, particularly of the capital, there to dream of a pastorally perfect past. The picture, then, was joyful on the surface, but melancholy in its deeper meaning.

Such, at any rate, was my interpretation: but was it true? Was I reading something into it that was not there, or at least that the painter had never intended? This was not a question of any great importance, of course, but it occurred to me every time my eyes fell on the painting, which was often. There was only one way to answer it: to ask the painter himself.

At the bottom right-hand corner of the picture was his signature: *Yé-Yé*. It sounded African, but it was also the name of a type of music in France that had enjoyed a brief vogue. Evidently the name was a pseudonym, which would make finding him more difficult.

The idea of trying to do so had formed in my mind well before the embargo had been declared by the supposedly angered world; and there is no better way of keeping ennui at bay than to engage on a quest that is at once difficult, absorbing and unimportant. The illusion of purpose is better than no purpose at all, and with little effort one can persuade oneself that illusion is reality and that unimportance is importance.

Once the embargo was announced, the attraction to me of the quest increased yet further. The prospect of arrival in a remote country from which return might for a while be difficult pleased me. I had several times in my life found that a complete inability for geographical reasons to communicate with my normal acquaintances and close associates was rejuvenating; and when my friends objected that it was dangerous to go at such a time, they only strengthened my resolve. Danger is the most powerful solvent known of all other cares, and once it is past adds to the stock of worthwhile memories. Of course, I speak only of danger that is freely chosen.

Even at the best of times it would have been difficult to find Yé-Yé. I had bought his picture at a small gallery in the country's second city, which was in the north of the country, a city still of colonial aspect, at least in its centre. I was uncertain that I should be able to find the gallery again, or even that it was still there to be found; and that, I need hardly add, was only the beginning of the difficulty. The naïve art of the country had not been exactly mass-produced, but neither was it wrung from a few tormented or tortured souls, easily identifiable by their unusual activity and way of life. The demand for this kind of art having fallen, and with it the ability of the country to import brushes and paints, or anything else, it was likely that many of the artists had abandoned their art and turned to other means of subsistence. In a country of such high mortality, moreover, it was far from impossible that – though I had imagined the picture to be that of a young man – Yé-Yé had died in the intervening decade. And if found, he might not be willing to speak to me or, if willing, unable to explain himself and his picture.

I was the only passenger on the last flight to the country. The aircraft had been sent to fetch people from it, not to take them there. It was a strange experience to have so large a craft to oneself, apart from the crew: they looked at me as if I were suffering from a communicable disease or were perhaps a dangerous madman who might turn violent at any moment. They resented serving me more than if I had been a full complement of passengers.

The island was shared between two countries, divided by a more or less straight line, on either side of which they spoke different languages and had, in the estimate of each, a superior culture to the other. The country to which I was destined had about a third of the total territory.

The border between them was one of those purely human artefacts that had become physical, geographical, almost geological. As you overflew it at many thousands of feet, you could see it as clearly as any line on a map. To one side the land was a lush tropical green, on the other a desert brown. Many of the inhabitants of the brown land went to labour in the green, where they were ill-treated and from time to time massacred: but necessity still drove them thither. This, too, was part of the background of Yé-Yé's picture, the emotional, historical and economic soil from which it grew.

After the usual difficulties at the airport, where the simplest matters entailed long and complicated negotiation, and the general atmosphere was one of civil disturbance rather than of organisation, I reached my hotel by means of a creaking taxi whose driver had won the contract to take me by a mixture of wheedling towards me and aggression towards others. By the way the taxi shook and jerked, it appeared to have square wheels, an impression created by bald flat tyres and potholes in the road.

The hotel was a famous one, in which all notable visitors (famed or infamous) to the country had stayed. It was not the most luxurious – there were one or two gilded and marble-clad establishments in the hills above the city where the sempiternal elite with some white blood still lived – but it was the most distinguished. It was wooden-framed, in the elaborate style favoured by the nineteenth century bourgeoisie of the country before it went Californian. It had deteriorated since my last visit, however, and had gone well past the charming genteel stage of decay. The garden was untended and had returned almost to scrub; the bushes were wild and there were cactus-like shrubs with leaves that ended in spikes so fierce that they might have served the Inquisition or the secret police as instruments of torture.

Guests being now so rare a commodity in the hotel, I expected to be warmly welcomed, but hardship and despair after former prosperity breed surliness and resentment at interference rather than warmth or eagerness to oblige: or perhaps it was the cannabis that the owner evidently smoked all the time (for it was he who eventually came to meet me after I clanged a wheezy bell) that dulled his wits and promoted his bleary-eyed indifference to the external world. He was a half-caste, of yellowish complexion rather than brown, suggesting that he rarely ventured out into the sun, admittedly unpleasant in the humidity of the place; his hair was done into dreadlocks of many years' development, slightly reddish but now grizzled with grey, that he seemed to think conferred upon him some superior wisdom or insight, as long white beards were once supposed to have done. He looked at me as if I were some kind of irritating epiphenomenon or uninteresting hallucination, an intrusion on his spiritual reverie. I judged him a man who had been reluctant to leave his rebellious adolescence behind, but who also had not the strength or resolve to renounce his material inheritance, the hotel having been handed down to him by his father and trapping him in his current life. He saw in every guest – now so few that there was little economic reward in attending to them - a symbol of the freedom that he lacked. His self-absorption prevented him from seeing that every man has his own chains.

As soon as I had deposited my things in my room, I went in search of a drink. There was a bar in the hotel, a high-ceilinged room with peeling paint and a large fan that revolved so slowly that it seemed more to provide a ride for flies than an attempt at cooling the room. Behind the bar was an old black barman with a whitish cotton shirt thinned by many washings, with a bow tie almost at the perpendicular.

There was one man at the bar. He approached me as soon as he saw me.

'Hi!' he said. 'When did you come into town?' He had the long drawl of the American Deep South, of Alabama or Louisiana perhaps.

'Just now,' I replied, and we shook hands.

'Sylvester, he said. 'Everyone calls me Silver.'

Our introduction over, he asked me what I would have.

'Not that there's much choice,' he said. 'It's rum or rum.'

I said that in that case I would have rum. The rum of the country varied between gullet-scouring firewater and the best in the world. My momentary companion – Silver – shouted his order to the barman who reacted with the obsequiousness of one obliged by his position to recognise no rudeness in others.

Before the rum was poured, I had time to examine Sylvester more closely. He was below average height, rotund, squeezed into clothes that were too tight for him, as if constriction were all that were necessary for him to lose weight. He had combed and plastered strands of black hair, possibly dyed, over his balding pate. I wondered what he saw when he looked in the glass.

The rum arrived.

'You've come at a good time,' said Sylvester. 'There's ice today.'

'Lucky?' I asked.

'Power outages,' he replied. 'And sometimes they don't get the hotel generator up and generating till the ice's melted. Sometimes it's because there's no fuel and sometimes because they're asleep.'

He had been here some time, then, long enough to disparage the locals.

He clinked my glass.

'To the embargo,' he said. 'Long may it last.'

I noticed then that it was not his first drink of the evening.

'To the embargo?' I asked.

'Sure,' he replied. 'It's good for business – my kind of business. There's nothing like import-export during an embargo.'

I suppose he must have taken my measure – that I was not some kind of official – for his confidence was indiscreet, to say the least.

He was a specialist in embargoes (breaking them), so to speak. They generated super-profits for those prepared to take the risks in breaking them. There was always at least one embargo going on somewhere in the world, usually more, as if the world needed to feel good about itself, to feel that it was conducted along moral lines. This was absurd, of course. Embargoes were power politics, nothing more. Embargoed countries were often no worse than others, just easier to kick around.

And did I know, he asked, what were the first items to be smuggled into an embargoed country? I assumed it must be something like oil or flour, or perhaps guns and ammunition.

'That's what everyone thinks,' said Sylvester. 'But they're wrong. It's pink champagne and single malt whisky.'

These were the commodities, apparently, without which no corrupt petty dictatorship could long function. Luxuries were necessities for those who wrought tyranny.

'And exports?' I asked.

'Refugees, mainly. I only arrange their consignment.'

The country had been accused of being a way-station for the international drug trade. I decided against asking for details.

'It must be risky,' I said.

'The stakes are high. We operate out of ....'

He named an island in the Caribbean in which they would have sold real estate to the devil himself. It was a coral speck in the sea on which hundreds of thousands of companies were registered. It would have taken fewer than ten armed policemen to overrun it, so it seemed that the world – in some sense or other of that overused word – wanted it to survive.

'And what brings *you* here?' he asked.

What indeed? Oddly enough, it had not occurred to me that he would ask and so I had no ready answer to give him. To tell the truth to such a man would have sounded absurd and probably implausible, a man who had swum in murky waters for so long that he must have assumed that all waters were murky. To such as he, all motives were ulterior (perhaps he was right). And indeed my story would have appeared strange if someone else had told it to me: juvenile or childish. There was no doubting that he lived in a grown-up world in which he did important, if dirty, work. I, by contrast, was merely diverting or indulging myself. His purpose was at least a tangible one ending with money in the bank, or wherever he kept it.

'I'm a tourist,' I said.

'Ha!'

It sounded even more absurd than that I was searching for an obscure artist with a false name whose picture I had bought many years before, merely to ask him what he had meant by it. Sylvester must have been convinced that I was up to something: I was a competitor in carpet-bagging, perhaps. I think he wanted to find out more, for next he asked me whether I would join him for dinner. He knew a place, he said, which was the only one where you could get chicken – if you could call it chicken. He was the kind of person who knew a place (the word *place* in this context had an almost technical meaning) everywhere he went, or soon found one.

11

It was not far. It was a kind of veranda that opened on to the street, protected by a strong wire mesh or grille on the street side. We were the only customers. It was hot, humid and airless, but slightly less intolerable outside than in. We ordered a kind of chicken-stew, a feast day dish in a country in which people mostly ate only to allay their hunger pangs. Sylvester made no attempt to meet the local languages – French or Creole – halfway, or with any recognition that not everyone was born to his own language, failure to understand which he took as a sign of perversity, stupidity or malice.

The chicken, he warned me, would be tough, with more tendon than meat. That was because chickens in this country were not fed but had to fend for themselves. They pecked in the dust or the mud for whatever they could find, which was not much, even though, like pigs, they would eat anything.

'Why this steel mesh?' I asked him.

'You'll soon find out.'

He was right. No sooner had the food been brought to our table than ten or fifteen small children appeared as if from nowhere. The proprietress, a fat lady in a country in which adiposity still indicated wealth, stood on the threshold of her restaurant to try to beat them away with a broomstick. Was her anger feigned or real?

The children were emaciated and in rags, mere tatters. The smallest of them managed to wriggle their thin wrists through the mesh and tried to reach the table to grab a morsel of food from our plates. Others managed only to get their fingers through, which then waved in the air like the tentacles of a sea anemone. This was accompanied by a constant chorus of whining supplication.

'Take no notice of them,' said Sylvester, putting a forkful of food inaccurately into his mouth.

Take no notice of them! How was such a heroic feat of disregard possible? It required a capacity for negative hallucination: not to see what was not there, but not to see what was. And yet it *was* possible, because Sylvester managed it. Noticing that I was rendered somewhat uneasy by the way he was the object of angrily envious glances each time he put something into his mouth, he said:

'You'll soon get used to it if you stay.'

I suspected not only that he had not taken long to get used to it, but that he even derived some pleasure from it. There is nothing like the misery of others to persuade oneself of one's own good fortune: thoroughly deserved, of course.

'Beats me why they keep having children,' he said, 'when they can't even feed them.'

I wanted to protest, but I knew that whatever I said would sound hollow even in my own ears. Poverty, ignorance, a desire for security in old age might explain it: yes, this was all very well, but surely the thought must have occurred to them at some stage that the getting of more children was not a good idea? To think, after all, was not only to be, *à la Descartes*, but to be human, and no one was absolved from the need to do so. But this seemed ungenerous and lacking in compassion, being the reaction of someone who had always had considerable power over his own circumstances.

But I knew from experience that entering a discussion on the side of the angels was futile or worse, and that one's vehemence when one did so was evidence of a nagging uncertainty about one's own argument. To blame a deeply impoverished man for anything was like kicking a man when he was down; but never to blame him for anything was to deprive him of his humanity.

'If you give them anything,' said Sylvester, 'the news'll get out and only attract more of them and start a fight among them.'

He was probably right. To give them a few scraps would solve nothing: and yet, if I were one of them, I would have wanted to be given some scraps to alleviate my hunger of the moment. One doesn't deny morphine to a man in deep pain because it won't cure the disease that causes it.

'In a country like this,' said Sylvester, 'you have to look after yourself first.'

'Is there any country in which you don't?' I asked.

Sylvester looked at me appraisingly. Was I a fool, or some kind of subversive do-gooder?

'Just see what happens,' he said.

He pushed a chicken bone out of the grille. A writhing, medusoid mass of little fingers grabbed at it. There was no honour among the hungry. The melee that followed made a rugby scrimmage seem like a military parade. There was much high-pitched screaming and shouting. Madame and a male assistant were attracted by the noise and lashed out with broomsticks to beat any child within range. They dispersed the children, one of whom must have had the chicken bone, for there was no sign of it on the ground afterwards when they had gone.

'See what I mean?' said Sylvester, after the successful conclusion of his experiment.

What was its moral, though? What did it teach?

'You can't feed them all,' said Sylvester, which was obviously true. Still, I did not (for the moment) find it quite as easy to dismiss the scene from my mind as he evidently did. I couldn't pretend that I hadn't seen it, or that it meant nothing to me. My quest for Yé-Yé, which had already cost a fortune unimaginable to these children, seemed wasteful, frivolous and self-indulgent in the face of such poverty. Perhaps it would have been better, at least for my peace of mind, if I hadn't come to the country and witnessed (or taken part in) this episode, for I could hardly un-see what I had seen.

Travel doesn't so much broaden the mind as harden the heart. It also stimulates rationalisation. Was it not the case, I reflected once back in the hotel and free of Sylvester's degrading company, that civilisation had always depended on, indeed had been created by, enormous differences in the fortunes of people? The glories of the Renaissance were built on the backs of Tuscan peasants. Of course, I could not claim for myself any role in creating or advancing civilisation by my quest: but even so (I thought), civilisation would collapse if all activity other than succouring the poorest were to cease. I knew that my argument was a form of self-tranquilisation, but it worked well.

I resolved to spend a couple of days in the capital before heading north. There were few sights of the guidebook kind in the city, but I had seen enough of such sights in my life for me to find other things more interesting, and one could hardly say that the streets of this city were uninteresting, even if hardly appealing to the aesthetically fastidious. It was by far the most impoverished urban agglomeration – by now it scarcely deserved any longer the name of city – in the western hemisphere, and probably among the most desperate in the world. When one compared it with pictures of fifty years before, one lost faith in the reality of progress. According to income statistics, it was even poorer then than it was now, but somehow it seemed less desperate in those days, more liveable. Was the peculiarly desperate nature of modern poverty an illusion, then, as if it were anomalous where once it had been natural? The city fifty years before had not pullulated then as much as now with an influx of destitute peasants at the end of their tether. In those days, the streets looked swept and even clean, and this was unlikely to have been because the photographers wanted them to appear so. Nowadays, you couldn't have pointed a camera (if you had dared to do so) without capturing for posterity the piles of rotting garbage in the streets being sifted by men, women and children, ulcerated pi-dogs and hopping vultures in the hope of finding some sustenance. Someone once told me that New World vultures were not *true* vultures, but they looked uncommonly like vultures to me.

Astonishingly enough, though, I had no feeling of personal danger as I walked these terrible streets, even though everyone must have known that I, *ex officio* as it were, must have had sums of money or belongings about me that would have secured their sustenance for weeks. Money changers, eager to change dollars into the local currency at many times the official rate, stood on street corners and waved their wads of banknotes bearing the portrait of the last dictator but three without any fear of robbery. What inner or outer compulsion kept order in this way?

My plan was to hire a car and drive to the north. Although the journey was not long in miles, I had no great expectation of the state of the roads and thought to stay overnight at a mission station about halfway where, on my previous visit, I had been welcomed and entertained for the night by an American medical missionary of whom, though I am far from religious, I retained admiring memories.

He was a remarkable man, though I confess to having had a prejudice against missionaries, especially Protestant (I preferred the Catholic ones, mainly for aesthetic reasons). In my adolescence I had read a biography critical of Albert Schweitzer, the great musicologist and doctor who immured himself in the West African jungle and who was an iconic hero at the time, as instantly recognisable as the other Albert of the epoch, Einstein. Such self-sacrifice, such love of humanity! But the biography maintained that his medical work was nugatory in its effect, his hospital in the jungle was dirty and disorganised, and his sacrifice was mainly that of his family - his wife and children − on the altar of his egotism. With adolescent glee and willingness to believe ill of all the world's heroes, I instantly believed what I had read, and it left a permanent residue in my mind as an instinctive hostility to Protestant missionaries, whom I came to regard as soapy hypocrites.

I had mellowed with age, no doubt, when I first met Dr Brown, but I still found it difficult to imagine a religious conviction so deep that a man would be willing to devote his entire life to persuading others of a different culture from his own of the truth of his beliefs, all the more so as a training in medicine is a training in scepticism.

But, surprisingly to me, I had found him a congenial man, not without a sense of humour. He had started his mission hospital from scratch, building it himself, albeit with funds from his native Kentucky. Before his arrival, there had been practically no medical attention available in that part of the country, if you discounted the practices of the voodoo adepts or priests who threw bones and smeared chickens' blood: all very well if your illness was psychological in origin or would heal spontaneously (the majority of human illnesses, after all), but quite useless against the serious diseases that were nevertheless very prevalent among the poor and killed them in large numbers.

I arrived at the mission the first time without invitation but received a warm welcome from him and his wife nonetheless. Perhaps I was the more welcome because they were very isolated and must have received very few visits from the outside world. They immediately asked me to stay the night, which I was glad to do.

The copious dinner of Kentucky farm food was excellent – people rarely emigrate from the cuisine of their childhood and youth – but there was, of course, no alcohol. Before the meal began, Dr Brown pronounced a grace while we held hands round the table with our eyes shut. This was a ceremony that I would normally have despised, but when Dr Brown said that he was grateful for the food we were about to eat, I think that he actually meant it. It was the first time I had ever heard grace pronounced with sincerity and not merely as a form of words, and I was, despite myself, moved by it. Perhaps it was easier to say grace and mean it when you had been treating malnourished children all day, as had Dr Brown: but I had the impression that he would have meant it just as sincerely in the midst of plenty. Whatever the rationality or otherwise of thanking a putative being of unknowable predilections for the fruits of human labour (and were we also to thank him for withholding those products from so many?), the attitude expressed by the grace, of taking nothing for granted, not even so much as a humble potato, seemed to me then what had not struck me before, a recipe for a deep kind of happiness. And

Dr Brown, at the time, was a happy man.

He was a good talker on many subjects. No doubt the flow of his words had been damned up for several months since his last visitor from the outside world. His wife, who provided the infrastructure of his life and activity as it were, was self-effacing in a fashion that would not, perhaps, meet with modern approval. Among other things, he was a self-taught archaeologist of some note and had even started a little museum on the mission site as a contribution to the culture of his adoptive country (to which he had come as a young man). He claimed to have discovered the exact place at which Christopher Columbus had first set foot on the island and thereby, according to a certain school of history, brought sin into it. How far Dr Brown's collection of shards of pottery and bits of rusted iron and so forth established the truth of his claim I was not in a position to say, but he was not the kind of man to make wild claims to discovery of his own. I offered no demurral and expressed no scepticism but said that the country must surely have been grateful to him for his researches. He smiled at my naivety.

'It couldn't have cared less,' he said.

'But…' I interjected.

'I tried to interest the government to protect the site and fund a better museum, but it wasn't interested and didn't see the point. On the other hand, it thought I was up to something, treasure-hunting, seeking for hidden gold, despoiling the patrimony. It forbade me to do any further research.'

I expressed my disapproval at so foolish and short-sighted a prohibition. I could see that in the circumstances of the country, even benevolent government, if such there had ever been, might have many other priorities than the uncovering of detritus half a millennium old, but actually to go so far as to prohibit others from searching…

Dr Brown entered into a disquisition on the national psychology and from there, by a natural progression, on to the belief system and ritual practices of the local population. Here he grew more serious, more grave. He thought them fit only for stamping out, though by persuasion rather than by force. They were, he said, of the devil. I did not care to start a discussion on the nature and quality of superstition compared with rational belief.

Yes, he said, human sacrifice continued, and even ritual cannibalism. Of course it was hidden, no one averred it openly, but it was still practiced all right. His wife nodded in agreement, enthusiastically I thought.

I was in no position to dispute it. He, after all, had lived in the country for more than thirty years, he spoke its language; I was but a bird of passage, overflying it on my way to… to where, exactly?

'But if no one admits it,' I asked, 'how do you know?'

'Children disappear. Albinos, for example.'

'One day,' said Mrs Brown, who until then had said very little, as if it had not been her place to speak, 'an albino girl came to us and begged us to take her in and protect her. She said that her brother, who had also been an albino, was taken and sacrificed. Her parents had wanted it.'

'What happened?'

'We took her in, of course. But one day not long afterwards, she disappeared and has not been seen or heard of since.'

'They live in a world saturated with magic,' interjected Dr Brown. 'They believe that everything bad that happens is the result of spells cast by witches and magicians who appeal to evil spirits. They seek protection by sacrifices.'

'That means they often come to Dr Brown too late to be cured,' said Mrs Brown, referring to her husband in the third person. 'When they fall ill, they go first to their witch-doctors to have a spell removed or neutralised.'

'They have a very complex belief system,' said Dr Brown.

'It's pure paganism,' said Mrs Brown. By now we were on to apple pie. 'It's impossible to find fresh apples here,' she said as she served it. 'I have to use canned.'

Dr Brown said the country would never advance while the old beliefs, a hangover from Africa, persisted.

'And what about zombies,' said Mrs Brown, 'tell him about zombies.' It was as if she wanted to convert me to some viewpoint of their own.

'When we arrived,' said Dr Brown, 'we'd heard of them, of course, but we thought they were a Hollywood invention. They're not, they really exist.'

'In what sense?' I asked. People, after all, may truly believe that they are possessed by the devil without being possessed by the devil.

'They are beings who are outwardly human but who have had their souls removed. They have no emotions and no facial expressions. They have the form of men but are like machines.'

'They're outcasts,' took up Mrs Brown. 'Unpersons. They wander on the edge of villages. They are supposed to have died, been buried and raised from the dead by the houngans, the voodoo priests.'

'Do you believe it?' I asked. After all, there was a faint analogy with the belief that they had come to the country to propagate, though of course it was an analogy that I did not draw.

'Fifteen years ago,' said Dr Brown, taking up the baton as it were, 'a man called Bienvenu Dorval was buried in the cemetery nearest here. 'I know because I treated him before he died, and I went to his funeral.' He paused in his recitation. 'I see him now from time to time wandering on the edge of the village.'

'The only way for him to die now, according to the locals,' said Mrs Brown vehemently, as if she were contemplating some kind of revenge, 'is with a stake through his heart or the cutting off of his head.'

'It is said that the houngans who raise them use them as slaves,' said Dr Brown. 'They don't have to be paid or even fed.'

'And is this true?' By my question, I hid my growing impression that the country had sent them mad.

'I haven't seen it myself.'

'But is it possible?'

Dr Brown did not answer directly. If he were mad, he was not so mad that he did not still appreciate what others might think if he revealed his true beliefs.

'Some years ago,' he said, 'a young researcher from Harvard came to investigate. 'He had long hair, wanted originally to be a rock star, I guess, but ended up as a scientist. He was searching for the drug that he thought put people into a state of suspended animation that would explain the phenomenon. He called himself an ethnobotanist. He was convinced that the houngans knew of a plant that could do it.'

'Did he find it?'

'He said he did.'

'There must be more to it,' I said, 'than an initial state of suspended animation. After all, the effect of the drug, whatever it is, must wear off. And you say the zombies walk around with no thoughts or will of their own for years.'

'Yes, it's their devilish beliefs that affect them,' said Mrs Brown. 'They take over their minds completely. The houngans deceive them. That's why we're here.'

'The truth,' said Dr Brown, 'the truth will set them free.'

The next morning, early, Dr Brown showed me his small museum, the pride of which was a piece of wood from the first European ship – if we discount the Vikings – to have reached the New World. Then he took me to his clinic which, as a doctor myself, I was interested to see. The waiting room, if such it could be called, was a large shelter with a corrugated iron roof supported on wooden poles. A small crowd, mainly of women and babies, had already gathered, some standing, some sitting on plain wooden benches. There was no question of privacy or confidentiality as Dr Brown went among them asking what was wrong. In that way, he could estimate who needed to be attended to first and most urgently. I had supposed that in so poor a country people would not attend a doctor for trivial complaints, but I was mistaken. Dr Brown winnowed them out with a practised eye, and I was about to remark that they were wasting his time when I bethought myself. In a country such as this, as in our own two centuries ago, the slightest malady might turn fatal in a matter of hours, and a minor injury turn to blood-poisoning. Life always hangs by a thread, no doubt, but it was by a far finer thread for these people. You couldn't blame them for being nervous at the first sign of malady.

Dr Brown told me that he did his surgical cases in the

afternoon. He had trained his wife to give the anaesthetic and he performed the surgery. I began to feel that I was now in his way, obstructing or slowing him down in his work, and I took my leave with my sincere thanks. He said it had been a pleasure and if ever I were passing this way again, I should be most welcome to call in on him and his wife. I felt that he meant it, that it was not merely a form of words.

'You'll still be here?' I asked.

'I intend to retire here and die here,' he said. 'This is my country.'

I found this moving. He uttered it simply, as a matter of fact, without posing as a hero. He was not trying to gain my admiration, though he had it. However alien the beliefs that had brought him here might be to me, there was no doubting his devotion to the welfare of the people, a devotion greater than I had ever felt or put into practice.

It is always a mistake to revisit scenes that have impressed you deeply. A cliché, no doubt, but as Dr Johnson said, we need more often to be reminded than informed. At any rate, my return was a mistake.

The atmosphere at the mission station had changed completely. There was an air of desperation about it which there had not been before. Dr Brown had aged by far more than the number of years intervening between my visits. He was now an old man, worn out not only physically but, I thought, morally and spiritually. He exuded an exhaustion that was more than that of excessive labour, though it was certainly the result of that as well. He was emptied of hope, almost of purpose beyond dealing with or surviving the present moment. He had always been busy with patients, but now he was overwhelmed by them. The crowd had become a tidal wave. He moved among those waiting for attention, amidst the cries and moans, like... well, like a zombie, a zombie whose sorcerer had ordered him to attend to the pullulating sick.

He was not pleased to see me again, rather the reverse. At first he did not recognise me, not even when I reminded him of my previous visit all those years ago. Eventually a vague memory stirred in his brain; and I was slightly put out because it is unflattering to one's self-conceit to remember better than to be remembered. Now I was an unwelcome intrusion or obstacle to a task that was in any case Sisyphean. He had told me on my first visit that his intention had been to hand over to another tiller of the field and devote himself more to his archaeological studies, but the absence of a replacement and the imperative needs of so many people had evidently prevented him from carrying out his plan. It seemed to me obvious that one day in the not distant future he would drop down dead in midst of his labours, and I sensed that he knew it too.

I therefore did not linger at the mission but continued on my journey to the north. As I did so, avoiding potholes, donkey carts and peasant women transporting bundles of twigs on their heads, I wondered what he had achieved in his more than forty years in the country. Perhaps in a century's time his discovery of the landing place of the first European ship (if further research corroborated it) would be recognised as a great service to the nation, but for the moment and the foreseeable future it was of little account. And while he who would do good must do good in minute particulars, there was no disguising the air of futility or defeat that now hung over his medical labours, which were as great as could have been demanded of any man. The tide of need had not receded and never would, at least not by the employment of his methods. He was trying to plug a volcano with cotton wool. His aim of slaying superstition, or at least of replacing it with a more benevolent one, had not been fulfilled. What could one man do against an immemorial tradition and the weight of a whole history? His project had been no more practical than if he had given everyone Descartes to read in the hope of converting them to rationality.

Why did everything seem so much more desperate now? Was it my perception or was it reality itself that had changed? The statistics, those supposedly infallible guides to reality, did not reflect the desperation, and even pointed to some slight improvement. Are we so wedded to the notion of inevitable progress that its absence strikes us as actual deterioration? Certainly, there is a modern feeling (from which I do not consider myself immune) that if you are not getting richer, you are getting poorer.

There was no question, however, that the state of the road, never very splendid, had greatly deteriorated. In one small town a pothole had opened up in it that had swallowed a small truck which, driving at night without lights, as was the custom, had fallen into it and had been the object of plunder rather than of rescue, little of it now remaining except a carcass, like that of a roast chicken picked clean. Rusting skeletons of small trucks and buses, overturned at strange angles, appeared at intervals by the side of the road. For the local people, as Dr Brown had told me on my first visit, accidents happened not because the vehicles were unmaintained, their brakes failing, their tyres bald, their drivers drunk, nor were so many people killed in them because they were so overloaded, with people clinging to them like shipwrecked sailors to a raft, but because of the malign magic practised by someone in the locality, or perhaps by a competitor of the owner of the crashed vehicle. The pressing problem after an accident, then, was to find the culprit, the person who had either cast a spell himself or paid for a spell to be cast. The likely suspect often fled, which of course proved his guilt. If he had been innocent, he would have waited to be killed.

On my way to the north, I decided to revisit for a couple of hours a little bay that had been used to receive passengers from cruise ships. The country even then had been of evil repute, though it was undergoing one of its periodic brief experiments with an elected government, albeit that the elections had been fraudulent and denounced by observers who delighted in the detection of fraud and found it everywhere. Cruise ships, gleaming white, would appear on the horizon from time to time, and weighing anchor nearer the shore, would discharge passengers in boats towards the bay, around which was a bluff that cut it off from any view of the country beyond and could therefore be isolated as safely as any isolation ward in a hospital. The turquoise waters sparkled, and the beach was raked and swept until it was as antiseptic as a Swiss clinic, a little pavilion set up where the landed passengers could refresh themselves with iced drinks as they gazed at the ship from whence they came. They stayed about thirty minutes and then returned. Such were the good old days.

I happened to be in the bay when a cruise ship arrived. Even at a distance it appeared vast, a sleek floating apartment block eight storeys high, no doubt arranged by hierarchy of price and luxury. Once anchored, it seemed to give birth to a progeny of little boats as if they would one day grow to the size of the mother ship. Once the boats had come within hearing range, or perhaps a little before, a local brass band gathered for the occasion struck up some jolly and slightly anarchic music, while drummers adopted a fixed grin of welcome. The barman at the pavilion got ready for his paroxysm of work. He hung up a notice to say that the ice had been made from sterilised water. I was unsure whether this would altogether reassure the approaching tourists.

The boats arrived in quick succession at a wooden jetty and the passengers struggled to alight, given a helping hand by several men employed for the purpose. Middle-aged and upward, most of the passengers were vastly fat, deprived of breath by almost any movement. The fatter they were, the gayer the colours they wore – baby pink, sky blue, apple green, corn yellow – and the more tightly they fitted their clothes, as if buying sizes too small were the same as losing weight. There was no magnificence in their obesity, as there is in that of some people who know how to carry it off.

No sooner had they landed than they waddled up to the bar for refreshment. They homed there like bees to a hive. Everything had been paid for in advance – it was included in the price of the cruise. They had to replace the fluid they had lost in getting as far as the pavilion. They were as avid for drink as if they had crossed a desert on foot.

One of them noticed me, a white man and yet not a passenger on the ship.

'Are you in charge here?' he asked.

Was this preparatory to some complaint about the arrangements, for example that there wasn't enough ice? A fat lady with dimples in her knees wailed that some sand had got in her shoe – bright yellow pumps – and someone should have warned her to wear walking shoes.

'No,' I said, 'I'm just visiting like you.'

'You mean, you're *staying* on Magic Island?'

Magic Island? What was he talking about?

'You think this is Magic Island?' I said.

'Sure, that's what the Tour Leader told us. This is Magic Island.'

Even in those days of relative calm, such was the country's reputation for disorder that the Tour Leader, whoever he was, no doubt acting on the orders of his company, did not dare tell the passengers in what country they were setting foot for fear of sowing panic. But how could anyone, let alone many people, believe that there was anywhere called Magic Island? Was that vast, gleaming ship at anchor – a technological marvel – a ship of fools? It was difficult to say which was the more marvellous, the brazenness of the lie or the credulity of those who believed it. And yet in some respects these people were the most sophisticated who had ever lived.

Should I tell them where they really were? I felt a certain (not entirely unpleasant) moral outrage at the deception that had been practised upon them. The fact that the buyer should beware doesn't absolve the swindler. Yet what purpose would telling them serve, other than a malicious glee in observing their alarm and spoiling their holiday (possibly, for some of them, that of a lifetime, the one that they had been promising themselves since the age of thirty), and possibly to the enrichment of some lawyers when they sued the tour company? Where ignorance is bliss, it is sadism to inform.

Having refreshed themselves with drinks that would only make them the thirstier and that were available on their ship anyway, the passengers returned to the jetty and the boats that took them back to the real world of the ship. I think they were relieved to go; they had never really wanted to come in the first place but had felt under some kind of obligation to do so, having come all this way, and now that they had escaped the adventure unscathed (except for one lady who had exclaimed that she had been bitten by a mosquito) were pleased to return to complete safety and comfort. They had displayed no curiosity as to what lay beyond this most untypical beach of Magic Island, more stage than landscape.

As I watched them depart, I was overcome, as I not infrequently am, by a sense of the futility of existence. So much human effort had gone into making that scene possible, and yet what did it amount to? Certainly, as soon as the passengers were gone and before the ship had sailed away with what seemed like a disdainful hoot, the band had packed up and dispersed, their grins wiped from their faces, and the barman directed a few labourers to carry away what remained of the drinks.

The bay was not far from my destination and I revisited it. It was not a long detour, but the little spur road that led to it was now so broken up that I negotiated it at hardly more than walking pace. I was surprised when I arrived at the bluff to find not only another car parked there, but a black Mercedes with smoked rear windows, the kind that ambassadors of poor countries to rich countries travel in. It was covered in a film of fine dust thrown up by the road, of course, but nevertheless remained a startling sight in the circumstances. Even more startling was that a man in a chauffer's uniform sat behind the wheel.

I made my way down the bluff to the beach. I saw at once,

without surprise, that the little pavilion, never very sturdy, was now a tattered ruin, which if seen for the first time would give little clue as to what it had once been. Scraps of bark hung from the remains of its wooden frame. But on what remained of its platform a man incongruously dressed in a dark business suit stood, as if wistfully, looking out to sea. As I approached, he turned to me. He wore dark glasses.

'Bonjour, monsieur,' he said.

'Bonjour.'

I joined him. The rhythmic sound of the wavelets breaking on the sandy shore was soothing. It gave the misleading impression that all was right with the world.

I have never been very good at starting conversations with complete strangers. As soon as I utter a word, it sounds banal, trite, empty; it drops like a stone from my mouth; it bores me, if not my interlocutor. The harder I search in my brain for something interesting to say, as I search in a drawer or a suitcase for something lost, the emptier my mind becomes.

'It's beautiful here,' I said to the man in the suit so inappropriate to place and climate. These dull words had taken me a considerable effort to formulate and utter.

'Yes,' said the man after a pause, as if he were labouring under the same difficulty. 'Our country is very beautiful.'

What to say next to this man, the presumptive owner of a Mercedes worth several times the income of a whole village? What first came into my mind – the poverty, corruption, injustice, tragi-comic history of the country – seemed wrong, for the man had clearly triumphed over them, if he were not either a beneficiary or a partial cause of them.

'It is a pity that no one comes,' I said.

'They are afraid.' There was another pause. 'And what are

you doing here, monsieur?'

Again, I could hardly reveal my quest for Yé-Yé. It would sound as unbelievable as it sounded absurd.

'I am a tourist,' I said.

My words had an effect on the man like a sharp pull on the strings of a puppet. He became animated.

'You are not a tourist,' he said. 'You are a hero.'

I felt more foolish than heroic, but perhaps the two states – foolishness and heroism - overlap.

'Yes, a hero!' He clapped me on the back. 'I am the Minister of Tourism. You are the first tourist I have met. You are welcome to our country.'

He proceeded to paint a flattering picture of my bravery and independence of mind in disregarding all the propaganda and false and exaggerated information spread about his country, and I began to think that perhaps I was a hero after all. A man can be a hero to himself, even if not to his valet. It was quite something to have a government minister to oneself. I fought against a tendency to self-congratulation.

The minister was a civilian, brought in by the soldiers to demonstrate that the business of restoring stability, law, order and prosperity, etc., that is to say the Government of National Salvation as it called itself, was not a military one alone, but civilian too; nor was it, as the newspapers abroad all alleged, an attempted seizure of the lucrative drug trade from the gangs that ran it. Would the minister, a professor of law at the national university, have agreed to join it if it had been?

He was touring the country, visiting tourist sites to estimate what was necessary to rehabilitate them for future tourists, who at the moment were about as likely to appear as fairies at the bottom of the garden. Rehabilitation! This was a country in which rehabilitation was necessary every few years, neglect and the tropical climate, if not deliberate destruction, having reduced everything to near-ruins in the meantime. The money for rehabilitation had always to be sought from abroad, of course, for there was never any at home: and then, if obtained, much of it disappeared without trace. Strangely enough, in the brief intervals when the country had a government that the donors of funds approved of, the previous failures of rehabilitation were forgotten and the whole cycle started again. I suppose it was testimony to the amnesia and self-importance of the donors.

I left the minister to his tour of inspection, carried out, no doubt, from the compulsion to do *something*. But how much of human activity arises from the same need?

I drove on towards my destination. Dusk was about to fall, and I grew anxious. My progress was slower than I had anticipated, and darkness supervened with clichéd tropical suddenness. The road, hazardous enough by day, was a kind of blind-man's-bluff by night, with potholes, vehicles without lights, donkey-carts and pedestrians, some of them swaying drunkenly, so that each hundred yards negotiated without mishap or disaster came as a relief. As I neared the city, its approach announced by the presence of a few stalls with guttering kerosene lamps, the road was suddenly blocked by a barrage of battered old petrol drums filled with earth and stones. A crudely hand-painted sign saying *Déviation* pointed to a track off to the right.

There was no explanation, of course. The track, which I was obliged to follow, made the former road seem like a super-highway. I feared a puncture at any moment, for the stones were sharp and the tyres were bald. The track was narrow, steep and with hairpin bends. I could easily imagine, though not see, the ravine on one side or the other of it into which it would be all too easy to plunge. I wondered whether the track could even bear the weight of my car, or whether it might not collapse under it and turn into a landslide. But what choice did I now have but to continue? I could not turn round and could hardly reverse down the track whence I came. Spending the night where I was did not appeal to me. Yé-Yé, if ever I found him, ought to be flattered by the trouble I had gone to.

I had to drive with a fierce concentration, like a pathologist peering down a microscope in search of a cancerous cell, the harbinger of death. The briefest lapse of concentration might be fatal: and, tired to begin with, I was now near to exhaustion. Very faint lights flickered on the hillsides, so that I knew that I was still heading for the city. Even suburbs in this country went unlit; they were not orderly extensions of the city, but impoverished villages come to town. I peered through my windscreen as through a glass darkly.

My progress was so slow that I was sorely tempted by impatience to accelerate whenever I could see more than ten yards ahead of me. Not knowing exactly how faraway the city was, I thought it might take hours to reach it at this pace. As soon as my foot hovered over the accelerator however, the instinct of self-preservation overwhelmed me. So I did want to live, after all! I desisted.

I was beginning to despair of finding a bed for the night when, having rounded a hairpin bend, I saw a few hundred yards away a well-lit building in a sea of light. It acted on me almost like an electric shock. The land around it appeared to be, of all things, a garden. As I approached a little nearer, I realised to my delight that it was a hotel, the *Hôtel Bavière*. How easily a superficial despair can give way to a strong but superficial joy! But what a strange apparition, a Bavarian hotel, or a hotel claiming the name of Bavaria, in such an unfrequented corner of the world!

The large garden that I had seen from afar was surrounded by a wire fence in a perfect state of repair that seemed here almost miraculous. I was now like a man in a desert who finds that his mirage of an oasis, as he supposed it, is real. There was a gate in the fence, just behind which was a sentry-box. When my headlights shone through the gate, a man in a kind of bellboy's uniform emerged. Opening the gate sufficiently to approach my car but not enough for me to enter, he came to my window, greeted me and asked what I wanted. I replied that I wanted to stay in the hotel.

He returned to the sentry-box and made some kind of enquiry by telephone. He then opened the gate and signalled for me to enter. I was relieved. What if, for any reason, I had been refused admittance?

I drove up to the hotel. The road under my wheels was now perfectly smooth. This felt like great luxury or relief after pain. The gardens, illuminated by floodlights planted in the ground, were perfectly cultivated and with an obsessive neatness. Hibiscus and other (to me) exotic flowering shrubs stood to attention at regular intervals and were shaded by palm trees straight as grenadier guards. Between the shrubs and trees was a lawn, neatly cut but of a coarser, broader-leaved grass than that of more temperate climes. It was like Yé-Yé's jungle taken in hand by a sergeant-major. Nature here had not been left to its own devices.

I drew up at the hotel entrance. Waiting for me at the top of the few steps leading up to the doors was a man with frogging on his uniform that contrasted strongly with his black face. Behind him stood two maids in sky-blue uniforms with bleached white aprons and lace caps. There was a young bellboy in a red uniform waiting to carry my case. That I was surprised – astonished – by all this, I need hardly say. I had almost to pinch myself to prove that I was not dreaming. It was as if all this had been arranged for my sole convenience, for there were, as far as I could tell from the absences of other cars, no other guests that night at the *Hôtel Bavière*.

The bellboy ran down the steps and opened my door for me. The man with frogging, whom I now saw to have curls of white scattered in his hair, and whom I judged to be a kind of majordomo, bowed to me as I reached the top of the steps.

'Good evening, monsieur. Can I help you?' he said.

'Do you have a room?'

'Certainly, monsieur. Fetch monsieur's luggage,' he said to the bellboy, or so I presumed, for he addressed him in the speech of the country, often called a patois but in reality a language of its own.

The hotel entrance (and, as I was to discover, the rest of the hotel) was spotlessly, almost aseptically, clean. It was furnished aseptically too, almost like a clinic in which bacteria had no chance of survival. There was not much adornment: the comfort was functional or ergonomic, as it were. But behind the reception desk was a picture of the Harz mountains.

'Will Monsieur want dinner?' asked the majordomo figure.

With the question came an access of hunger. Until then, I had been like a man injured in battle who feels no pain until he has been removed from the battlefield. My hunger returned with a bed for the night.

'Yes,' I said. 'If it is possible.'

'It will take half an hour to prepare, monsieur. I apologise for the delay, but there are no other diners tonight.'

A whole machinery was being clanked into gear for my convenience, it seemed. I felt that the universe was not entirely indifferent or hostile to me.

The majordomo showed me to my room, a humble task that he let fall would normally have been performed by others whose night off it was. The room was furnished with a kind of luxurious simplicity; there was everything there a man needed who was used to his own company and capable of occupying himself with his own thoughts, but not more. There was something almost monastic about it, which suited my mood perfectly.

I went to the hotel dining room at the appointed time. It was a large hexagonal room between the two wings of the building. There were several tables, each of them covered with a brilliant starched tablecloth. The extent to which the sight of the table linen lifted my heart took me by surprise. Was I so attached, then, to the minor manifestations of my own way of life? Though I had not been in the country long, it was as if I were returning after a period of exile. The cutlery and glasses had been arranged with a care and attention to symmetry that suggested that someone had supervised the arrangement and attached great importance to it: an odd scale of values, when you came to think of it, in such a country. But there was something noble in the struggle against the country's natural tendency to entropy.

One of the women in the sky-blue uniform with white apron showed me to my predestined table. She looked as though she thought I might eat her. She spoke not a word: if she had tried to speak, I think her throat would have been paralysed by fear.

It occurred to me that, even in childhood, I had never experienced such a fear of others, a fear that was an entire stance towards life, so to speak, a manifestation of a sense of inexpungable inferiority.

Not surprisingly in the circumstances, there was no choice offered in what was brought to the table. Soup and beer appeared at the same time. The beer had condensation on the outside of the glass, a sign of functioning refrigeration. I was pleased and relieved. I knew all about warm beer in a hot climate from travels in Africa.

As I waited for the next course, a tall elderly white man entered the dining room. I guessed his age to be about seventy-five. He walked slowly towards my table. He had a slight limp.

'Bonsoir, monsieur,' he said, with a faint bow.

'Bonsoir.'

'May I join you?'

'Please do.' I signalled to him to take a seat. He sat down carefully, precisely.

'Would you prefer that we spoke in French, German or English?' he asked, in the last of these three languages.

'English,' I said.

He spoke with a marked German accent, but without grammatical error or shortage of vocabulary.

'I hope you are comfortable?' he asked.

'Very,' I replied. 'Thank you.'

'I am the proprietor. It is a matter of honour for me that my guests should be comfortable. Which is not easy – in the circumstances.'

I laughed a little, and a little wintry smile played on his mouth.

'I trust you had an uncomfortable journey coming here?' he

said.

'It was not altogether easy.'

'Nothing is easy in this country.' He paused for a moment. 'I have already dined,' he resumed, 'but do you mind if I join you in a beer?'

'Not at all. Delighted.'

Indeed, I was pleased. I like my own company well enough, but I am no hermit or anchorite.

The proprietor of the *Hôtel Bavière* ordered his beer by means of a nod and it was brought quickly.

'What brings you here?' asked the proprietor.

'Well,' I said, 'I'm a doctor but also a writer, and I'm on a strange quest.'

It was not so much that I felt that I could confide in him as that, being local, he might be able to help me with my enquiries.

'What is it?'

I told him about the painting by Yé-Yé I had bought years before and how I hoped to meet him.

'Yé-Yé is not a real name, of course,' he said. 'Here they take names and then abandon them with the same ease. Finding your Yé-Yé will be very difficult. It will be like searching for one fish in a shoal.'

'Perhaps I could find him through the art gallery from which I bought the picture,' I said. 'I remember that it was run by Lebanese.'

'The Nasir family,' said the proprietor. 'They are very well-known, of course. But their gallery is closed for the time being because of the situation and most of them have returned to Beirut – for safety.'

'Beirut for *safety*!' I exclaimed. Beirut at the time was going through one of its periodic episodes of destruction. 'Things must be bad here.'

The proprietor looked me intently in the face.

'They are, they are.'

It was not just a matter of shortages, he explained, though they were severe enough. But to those one might adapt, much of what we believe to be essential being superfluous at best. There was a certain pleasure to be had in making do with little: it gave rise to a sense of achievement. But extortion, threat, blackmail, theft, abduction and murder as everyday occurrences were not so easily adapted to.

'You are not afraid?' I asked.

'They leave me alone.'

I did not ask why. I thought the question might have been too intrusive for the beginning of an acquaintance and cause him discomfort. I asked instead how he thought I might go about finding Yé-Yé.

'There are still one or two sellers of paintings who don't have galleries but try to sell paintings at the side of the road from corrugated metal shacks. Their business is nearly dead, of course, but they might know.' He paused again. 'But in my opinion, I think your search is hopeless. Yé-Yé might have been Yé-Yé only for a day because he liked the sound of it, or it might have been because that's what a dealer wanted him to sign himself.'

I knew that he was right, of course, and in a sense had always known it. From the first, my journey had been frivolous, certainly unconsidered. But whenever one describes something as pointless, one is faced by the question of ultimate purpose: which I, for one, have never been able to answer. Whim is not the cause of, but the answer to, pointlessness.

I decided, almost as a substitute for finding Yé-Yé, to ask the proprietor of the *Hôtel Bavière* whether he thought my interpretation of his painting was correct or at least plausible: whether the feelings I had projected into it were to be found in the population. He took a sip of beer before answering.

'I think,' he said, 'you must remember that your Yé-Yé was, or is if he still exists, not an artist in the proper sense – not in the sense that we Europeans mean it.'

'What would you call him, then?'

He thought for a moment and breathed in deeply, as if taking mental sustenance from the air.

'At the time you're talking about,' he said, 'there were hundreds, perhaps thousands of young men in this country painting pictures such as yours for the tourist trade. No women, of course.'

'Why not?'

'Babies and finding charcoal to cook the one meal of the day. It was the men who earned money, if there was any to be earned.'

He took another sip of beer.

'It is not possible that hundreds, or thousands, of these people' – he swept his arm round the restaurant as if it were a microcosm of the whole country – 'could suddenly have become artists or discovered a burning need to express themselves.'

'Did not something like that happen before, of course at a much higher level, in Italy and the Low Countries?'

He could not disguise a snort of derision.

'You cannot extract from people what is not in them.'

'You mean, their history prevents it?'

'More than that, something much deeper than history. After

all, our history is a reflection of what we are. We get the history that we deserve, or at least are capable of.'

He took another sip of beer, like a punctuation mark or paragraph break.

'No, at the time, painting in this country had become a way of earning money. At its best it was craft, not art. Families like the Nasirs seized their chance: they saw that there was a vogue for the primitive in Europe and America, among people who were tired of civilisation. The mood was for something less disciplined, more spontaneous, or what they thought was spontaneous. They didn't see the Nasirs distributing the acrylic paints and canvases. They wanted the exotic too, preferably tropical, and mysterious too. Paintings from this country fitted the bill perfectly – for a time. Then, of course, the fashion changed, as fashions do, and the artists, so-called, returned to whatever they were doing before they took up painting, which was mainly nothing.'

'I don't think this necessarily means…' I was about to say that the conditions which called the paintings into being did not automatically deprive them of artistic merit or purpose – had not Yé-Yé displayed an instinctive sense of colour and composition? – but the proprietor cut across me: not from rudeness but from the urgency of what he had to say.

'Your Yé-Yé,' he said, 'was almost certainly given a model to follow. His work was not original, it was a copy. There would be ten or twenty or more copies, not all by him.' As if by way of consolation, he added, 'Of course, you can still enjoy it if you like it.'

There was a sting in the consolation, of course, namely that to like it was an error of judgment, a lapse of taste, or even a manifestation of mental or moral weakness.

'The Nasirs and others paid for everything during the boom period. It was an industry, mass production. Demand created the supply.'

'You assume,' I said, 'that there is a clear distinction between what is art and not art.' (I heard myself intoning an argument that in all other circumstances I despised. I even quoted Bishop Butler.) 'Everything is what it is and not another thing. I mean, everything is beautiful according to what it is, not according to whether it fulfils some abstract criterion. Originality has nothing to do with it.'

'But what an artefact *is* depends on its history and how and for what purpose it was made.'

In my heart I agreed with him, though I persisted in pretending not to do so. After all, who if given the choice of an original picture and a copy would not opt for the original, even if the original and the copy were indistinguishable? However difficult it might be to justify this preference on purely rational grounds, it has been the common prejudice of mankind for centuries: and who was I to set myself up against mankind?

'I know this country and its people,' said the proprietor. 'They are capable of imitation but not of art.'

'Not the highest art, perhaps,' I said. 'Though genius sometimes emerges from the most unexpected places. But still…' I tried another track. 'At the same time as I bought the picture by Yé-Yé, I bought one by a different painter. It was of a rural school with children playing in the yard. A teacher is supervising them as they play. The children, all boys, wear neat uniforms. There are green hills in the background. The national flag flies from a flagpole in the yard. The picture was painted during the period when the dictator had changed the flag from blue and red to black and red. But between the edge of the flag and the flagpole the painter painted a little patch of blue, not the blue of the sky but the blue of the old flag. I didn't notice it at first but saw it only on closer inspection. It must have been a subtle protest against the dictatorship.'

'But protests against dictatorship, however subtle, or cowardly, do not by themselves make art.'

'What I mean is that the paintings of the time were not just industrial products that meant nothing more to their producers. They put their own thoughts and feelings into them. No one would have told the painter to have put that little patch of blue next to the black of the dictator's new flag.'

'No doubt you are right, but that little variation does not make him Durer.'

How hard a life it would be, how discouraging of effort, if everything we did were always to be compared to the highest achievement in the field! There would have been no music after Bach, no painting after Rembrandt, no poetry after Shakespeare. Great works would intimidate rather than inspire. It struck me as odd that the proprietor should be so aesthetically demanding or fastidious in the circumstances of the country. Surely it was not the art that was actually produced, but that art should have been produced at all, that was a manifestation of the human spirit?

'As to the protest to which you refer,' continued the proprietor, with the precision of someone who has learned a language perfectly that he does not use often, 'it was, as you say, subtle, so subtle, in fact, as to efface itself. It salved his conscience, perhaps, but it did nothing else. The dictatorship endured his patch of blue.'

'Must everyone be brave and risk his life?'

'Not everyone *can* be brave, that is by definition, otherwise what counts as being brave would merely be shifted in the direction of what is now called foolhardiness. If everyone is brave, no one is brave. Bravery would not be exceptional. We would not notice it.'

The proprietor was evidently something of a philosopher, and I have always enjoyed long and inconclusive discussions about questions that are important and unanswerable. They take one's mind off the irritating small but pressing problems of daily life. The philosopher-proprietor leant forward.

'To protest against dictatorship in this country is to protest against its existence as a country.'

'What do you mean?' I asked.

'This is a country that can neither govern itself nor is worth being governed by others.'

'Why is that?'

'People get the government they deserve. The government reflects their soul.' Again he paused. 'You have studied the history of this country?'

'A little.'

By that I meant that I knew more of it than might have been expected of my countrymen, but my reading in it was desultory and went in spurts. I did not want to claim any more expertise than that. But the strange thing was that, once you had visited the country, your interest in it could be rekindled at any time, by an event in the news (almost always a catastrophe), a newly-published book, or an exhibition. As a result, I had over the years read quite a number of books about it. It was strange, this grip on the imagination that the country exerted: it was, after all, not of the slightest account in world affairs and if it disappeared under the sea the fact would not be registered on history's seismograph, the stock markets go up or down, not by so much as a blip. But perhaps it was its ever-present tragic dimension that was the cause of its hold, serving as a permanent reminder that disaster is never far away.

'Then you will know,' said the proprietor, 'that at no time in its two hundred years of existence as an independent country has it ever been able to organise itself in a semi-reasonable way.'

This could hardly be denied. Kings, emperors, marshals, generals, presidents-for-life, all self-proclaimed, succeeded one another like Banquo's descendants in Macbeth's imagination: except that none of them was wise, almost all of them were overthrown, and not a few were torn limb from limb by an enraged mob. On the other hand, they were a colourful lot. Dullness was not among the vices of the country.

'Yes,' I said. 'That certainly seems to be the case.'

'And why do you think it is?'

I suspected that the usual explanations would not meet with his agreement or approval: the legacy of slavery, the racial conflict that had always pitted those with European blood against those without, the world economic system and so forth.

'You have a much greater knowledge of the country than I.' By this answer I committed myself to nothing. And in fact I had no theory of my own to propound. I deemed it was better, more tactful, to sit at his feet. I doubted that he would mind this in the least.

'The people,' he said. 'You cannot get out of them more than is in them. You cannot make bricks from straw alone.'

I had finished my knuckle of pork with potatoes. It would

have been good for a winter's evening.

'They need always someone to tell them what to do,' resumed the proprietor. 'On their own they cannot plan, they cannot organise, they cannot maintain.' He swept his arm around the room once more. 'All this,' he said, 'needs constant supervision or it would fall into ruins in a week. I have to check everything daily, or it would become like everything else in this country, wreckage. They are still mining the bricks and stones from the plantation buildings they destroyed two centuries ago.'

'It must take a lot of work,' I said, referring to his prevention of the ruination of the *Hôtel Bavière*.

'I have built it up, I do not want to see it destroyed.'

But what was it all for? The effort to achieve something that made little or no difference was immense.

'We must strive for perfection,' he said, 'or we descend to the animal.'

'You have certainly chosen a difficult place to perfect,' I said as drily as I could.

'I cannot say that I like it,' he said. 'But it was my destiny.'

'How so?'

'I was born in this country, though I am not really of this country, at least not in any sense that counts. What is it that your Duke of Wellington said about being Irish? To be born in a stable does not make you a horse.'

'But how come you were born here?'

'We came here after the war,' he said. 'The first war, that is. I was only just born. My father was disgusted by the situation in Germany, by the political manoeuvring, the betrayal and corruption, and of course the growing immorality and decadence. He wanted to create something, to start again, to feel in charge.'

'In charge of what?'

'In charge of his life. Of something bigger than himself. He started a coffee plantation because at that time, before all the trees had been cut down for charcoal, the hillsides were good for coffee (the bushes need shade). It was very hard at first, but he succeeded. What was needed was organisation and my father had been an officer in the army.'

'You were raised, then, on the plantation?'

'Yes.'

'You went to school here?'

'At first my mother taught me, but when I was twelve, I was sent back to Germany. My father thought there were no schools in the country good enough, and he was probably right. He wanted me to grow up German. He wanted me to go to university there. He was a patriot.'

'You must have been at school during the rise of Nazism?'

'Yes, but I was more interested in Latin and physics. And sport, of course. Later, in girls.'

I imagined he would have been a handsome young man. Even now, he was distinguished-looking, his silver hair swept backwards in orderly fashion.

'Did you return?'

'The war came. I was at university. Of course, I couldn't finish. I was called up. Anyway, I couldn't have returned, because this country was on the other side, not that it had anything to do with it. But all German property in the country, including my father's plantation which he worked so hard to establish, was confiscated. It went completely to ruin straight away. That is justice, what they call justice!'

He gritted his teeth to control his anger.

'After the war? Obviously, you survived.'

'After the war, Germany was again in ruins, worse than after the first war. I came back to this country. My father had been released by then, having been interned and sent to America. By then there was peace, and he tried to get his property back. Of course, it was hopeless. He had been punished for being German. Anyway, by then he was too old and broken to start again. He died of a fever.'

'But you were still young and vigorous?'

'Yes, I thought I could make a better future here. Ha!'

His exclamation was mirthless and bitter. In his little verbal explosion, he expressed the waste, or what he thought was the waste, of fifty years of life.

'After the war, for a short time, this country seemed destined to be the next Cuba, a playground for rich Americans. I built this hotel. Politics soon destroyed everything, but I survived.'

'How?'

'I had friends in Germany who would send money when necessary.'

'Were you married?'

'Yes, I found a wife on a trip back to Germany. It was almost arranged for me. She died twenty years ago.'

'I'm sorry.'

'The medical conditions in this country are not good. If the diseases don't kill you, the doctors will.'

'And your children?'

'They are in Germany. They have much better lives there. One is a teacher and the other an engineer.'

'Do they come to see you?'

'Not often. They do not like it here. Too many frightening memories.'

'So you go to see them?'

'I am too old. It's far and not easy. They have their own lives to lead.'

'How sharper than a serpent's tooth is it to have a thankless child.'

'That is the modern world.'

Wearily, the proprietor of the *Hôtel Bavière* rose to go.

'I thank you for your conversation,' he said. 'It is not often these days that I have the opportunity to speak to a man of my own race and civilisation.' He bowed slightly, inclining his head stiffly. 'I wanted to study philosophy at university, but fate decreed otherwise. Most people I meet are interested only in their own affairs of the present moment. It has been a pleasure, an honour, and a relief, to meet someone who is interested in something beyond his own immediate life. This is rare.'

I had not thought of myself as an idealist before, rather as an egotist, but I was more than willing to accept his compliment. It warmed me inside, and there is nothing like a compliment to create a bond of sympathy.

'Good night,' I said. 'It has been a pleasure for me too.'

He inclined his head again, turned and limped away. A lonely man, obviously, and intelligent and cultivated, in need of conversation appropriate to his intellectual level. I flattered myself, almost, that I had done a good and charitable deed in coming here. Not long after he had gone, I left the restaurant and retired to bed to read for a time one of the great novels of the country, by a founder of its Communist Party who died young, possibly (it is said) of poison. I had read it before, when it moved me by its depiction of the dignity of the peasantry despite the hardship of their lives. Now the dignity was gone, leaving only the hardship. In the modern world, impoverishment heaps humiliation on the heads of those who suffer it. But the author did not pretend that his was a golden age. He has one of the peasants say:

No, God, you are not good, it's not true that you're good, it's a lie. We beg you to help us and you don't listen. Look at our pain, our hardship, our tribulations. Are you asleep, God, are you deaf, are you blind, God, are you without feeling? Where is your justice, where is your pity, where is your compassion?

Men have been asking these questions for centuries; I fell asleep.

The next morning, I went to breakfast. Pork knuckle increases your appetite the day following.

As I was finishing my papaya – the one fruit I detest, it is scented like a cheap boudoir – the majordomo sidled up to me.

'Excuse me, monsieur,' he said, 'if I interrupt. M. *le propriétaire* asks if you could be so good as to visit him in his office after you have finished your breakfast.'

'Certainly,' I said. 'With pleasure.'

'M. *le propriétaire* asks that you do not hurry but come at your own convenience. It is not urgent.'

When people say there is no urgency, they mean it is serious. What, I wondered, could it be?

'When you have finished, I will show you the way,' said the majordomo.

I hurried through breakfast. The majordomo was waiting for me at the door of the restaurant and I did not want to keep him waiting. He led me the way to the proprietor's office.

He was sitting at his desk. As one might have expected, it was very neat, the few papers arranged very carefully. To my surprise, though, there was a stethoscope laid out on it. The proprietor saw my surprise.

'I have a stethoscope in the same way as I have a generator,' he said. 'Here you cannot rely on anyone for anything.'

'Even doctors?'

'Even doctors. Often their stethoscopes have been stolen and they cannot afford to replace them.' He paused. 'Thank you for coming, doctor,' he said. 'I have a little health problem.'

He told me his symptoms. He was tired, he was short of breath if he walked too far, he couldn't exert himself as had always been his custom. He was not a man to complain lightly, or to exaggerate.

'I will have to examine you,' I said.

Strangely enough, there was a couch in his office. Normally, he said, he used it to take a half-hour siesta. It doubled his efficiency, he added, as if he had to excuse himself to me. In this climate one is at one's most vigorous only for a short time, immediately on waking. It was more logical to sleep, then, than battle through tiredness.

I asked him to strip to his underclothes. He was lean and sinewy rather than muscular, like a chicken that has spent its life pecking in the dust. For his age, his skin did not hang loose, so I guessed that he had neither lost much weight nor had ever been fat.

After a few preliminary examinations, I began to sound his chest. On the inside of his left upper arm was a tattoo in large Gothic lettering: *AB*.

'What is that?' I asked, though I already knew.

'My blood group,' he replied. 'During the war it was compulsory to have it done, in case we were wounded, unable to speak, and needed a transfusion. It saved time and lives.'

He did not appear anxious: he assumed my ignorance, as someone born after the event. But I happened to know that not every German soldier had had to have his blood group tattooed on his arm: only the SS. Moreover, it was only towards the end of the war that the SS were conscripts, having previously been exclusively volunteers. In the middle of the war, furthermore, the lettering in which the blood group was tattooed was changed from Gothic to Latin. He had been an enthusiast.

I said nothing. I continued my examination as if I had no swirl of thoughts or feeling. Sometimes one can think along two or even three lines simultaneously, and I began to review our conversation of yesterday in the light of a new understanding. It was possible, for example, that his sons did not visit him not through a distaste for the country, but through a distaste – to put it undramatically – for his past. Perhaps he did not return to Germany not because it was too far, but perhaps because - with time, paradoxically – it had become too dangerous. Perhaps he had always received, still received, funds from old comrades as a signal of solidarity, of keeping the old flame burning. Perhaps he had left – fled - Germany after the war not in search of better opportunity but to save his skin. He must have left early and felt safe in this country, or he would have had the tattoo removed – though of course that too would have been obvious to pursuers.

'I think you are in heart failure,' I said.

'What does that mean?' he asked.

I told him as I would have told any other patient. By doing so, I felt I had scored a kind of moral victory over him: for it is a doctor's creed (or ought to be) that he does his best for whomsoever comes before him, in direct contradiction to the creed in which the proprietor must have believed and on which he must have acted, namely that evil done to certain people was good, even the highest good.

Had he now come to another opinion? Had he changed? Did he feel regret, remorse, guilt? Pride, perhaps? And even if he did feel regret, remorse or guilt, what could or did they weigh in the balance? What was done was done; the murdered cannot be resurrected.

My examination completed, my recommendations made, I left the *Hôtel Bavière* abruptly. Had the proprietor never asked me to examine him, I might have spent several evenings in his company talking philosophy, so to speak, and congratulating myself on having found a person in such circumstances with whom to do so. There is (I have found) few greater pleasures than a community of taste in a far-flung place.

I departed without taking my leave. I did not even tell the proprietor that my mother, as a young woman, had fled the regime of which he had been an enthusiastic servant, and had never seen her parents again.

CREDULITY

To arrive in one country on the verge of collapse may be regarded as a misfortune; to arrive in a second looks like a choice.

As indeed it was. In those days I had not yet lost my taste for danger, and it was more than possible – indeed, it was likely – that the most vicious guerrilla movement in a continent of guerrilla movements would overthrow the government at any moment. Then the rest of the world would wring its hands and say, 'Never again!' – again.

Not only had I still the taste for danger but, though not even then in first flush of youth, I had the young man's sense of invulnerability and that the possibility of death somehow did not apply to him. At the same time, the advantage of danger, that it empties the mind of whatever other unpleasant preoccupations it may have been possessed of or by, remained. I courted danger without being in the slightest brave.

I had come to the country at the behest, or rather with the agreement, of a newspaper, to whom I had proposed the journey. I had taken time off, and it was an odd choice of holiday destination. The danger not only cleared my mind of other matters but gave to it a deep if illusory sense of purpose: I have never been able to undertake a journey just for the pleasure of it, for to have done so would have left me with a sense of futility. In this case I thought the world must be informed of the cataclysm, the holocaust, in preparation, and I was the man to do it. I knew, of course, that reports of impending cataclysms in far-away countries of which we knew nothing were no sooner read than forgotten, and that they created nothing more than slight ripples on the surface of the village ponds of our minds, but I was able to persuade myself that what I was doing was of capital importance. At least the world would not be able to say afterwards that it had not been warned, that it had known nothing, that it was taken unawares and by surprise.

There was a blackout when I landed. The revolutionary guerrilla movement had decreed a general strike, a cessation of all economic and other activity, obedience to its decree being enforced by what it called 'people's justice,' that is to say murder: and when the movement threatened to murder, especially defenceless unarmed citizens, everyone believed it. It had at least the courage of its brutality. No one could accuse it of hypocrisy in this regard.

The blackout was part sabotage, part threat. A large power plant had been blown up the day before my arrival, as had many of the pylons bringing current into the city. But the movement had also let it be known, by poster and clandestine radio station that it was every person's revolutionary duty to listen to, that the use of any electric apparatus in the home, for light or otherwise, whether from the public grid or from the private generators that every middle-class household now possessed, would be regarded as counter-revolutionary activity and punished as such. Moreover, the 'executions' ordered by the movement were carried out to inflict the maximum suffering before death on the victims, as what it called a 'revolutionary example'. Sadism was now a mark of ideological purity.

It wasn't easy to reach the city. Few were the drivers willing to brave the movement's interdiction, but few also were the passengers. The danger was such that the price was high, though surely not high enough to have been worth dying for. My driver was a middle-aged hothead: he would rather have had his throat cut (the movement's favoured *coup de grâce*), he said, than submit to tyranny. Besides, he had five children still to feed and could not afford to miss an opportunity like this. But if the fare, at ten times its normal rate, set a low price for a driver's life, so it did for the passenger's: for it was inconceivable that the movement, dedicated to the achievement of the most radical equality, would kill the driver but spare the passenger.

The journey into the city was that of the blind driving the blind, or very nearly so. One sensed rather than saw the shanty towns that had mushroomed on the low hills through which the road passed, and to which so large a part of the population had fled. They were faintly silhouetted as a slightly different shade of black against the black of the sky. It was a moonless night and the stars were extinguished by pollution. Not so much as a flicker of light emerged from a landscape in which millions lived. Here was another embargo that was a success.

Although it turned out to be without incident, the journey, as through a long, unlit tunnel, was exciting and kept me on the edge of the seat. Every yard advanced without having had one's throat cut was some kind of achievement. We were passing through the Valley of the Shadow of Death, but in my case without any rod or staff to comfort me. At least it was not boring, however, and the evasion of boredom was one of my greatest aims in life, as perhaps it was of everyone else's. It reminded me as forcefully as possible that in the midst of life we are in death.

The grandest hotel in the city was bathed in floodlight, as bright in the surrounding gloom as magnesium burnt in oxygen. Was this defiance, bravery, foolhardiness or security? No doubt it made it an easy target of rocket or bazooka attack, but there was a sandbag fortress around it and the lower windows were sandbagged. There were successive roadblocks around it manned by soldiers in camouflage and wearing black balaclavas. As we approached them, they held their hands, palms forward, to signal us to slow down and stop: on the slightest suspicion, they would have opened fire, for they were as jumpy among all their sandbags as sand-fleas. Probably we were in as much or greater danger from them as from the revolutionaries.

They shone powerful torches into the back of the car where I was sitting and quickly persuaded themselves that I was not a terrorist. Physiognomy is not an exact science, but everyone relies on it.

It was as if, next morning, a dark storm had cleared. The so-called strike was over, the people emerged as if they were small animals coming out of their burrows after a predator had passed by. They sniffed the air, so to speak, for their safety was only relative; the movement could, and did, strike anywhere and at any time. It regarded no one as innocent who had not joined its ranks: at best, non-members were *objectively*, as it put it in its revolutionary *langue de bois*, collaborators and therefore legitimate targets of a revolutionary justice that knew no penalty other than death. For the moment, though, it could not kill everyone at once. Full purification would have to await its final victory.

The money-changers were out in force, hundreds or even thousands of them. They held thick wads of banknotes aloft and waved them at passers-by. The old currency had been changed for a new, at the rate of a thousand million to one, in the hope that by the removal of nine zeros inflation would be tamed. This was like trying to control an epidemic of cholera by prohibiting the publication of news about it. The printing presses were still rolling, and the exchange rate fluctuated by the hour, usually downwards but sometimes with little spikes in the other direction. It was possible to lose a tenth of your money in a few minutes, and in any case the local money was now used only in the most trifling of transactions (for the making of which, however, it was still necessary). How the money-changers learned of the fluctuations in the rate was a mystery – this was in the era before instant universal communication – but it was clear that somehow they did. They were like a flock of birds that suddenly changes direction as it flies in the sky, as if under perfect orchestration. Rumour is the most powerful force in the world.

I did not stay long in the capital, for I had promised a newspaper that I would report from the isolated provincial city in which the movement was founded, and the money it had advanced me would soon run out. It was not much considering the risk I was taking, but I was expendable, and though I thought my venture of the greatest importance the newspaper had been reluctant to fund it at all. It had other fish to fry, such as the exposure of footballers' marital infidelities. For myself, I hoped not to lose too much money by my quixotic journey.

The mountain city was almost cut off from the rest of the country by the surrounding guerrillas. It was, in effect, under military occupation. It was reachable only by air, and it was a matter of time, so said the experts, before the movement acquired anti-aircraft weapons and shot down a passenger plane containing those who were, *ex officio*, class enemies. It had already put an end to travel by bus, the overcrowded transport of the poor: it halted buses at roadblocks and hacked the passengers to death with machetes. It did not take long for both the bus operators and passengers to get the message.

The city was the capital of the poorest province of a poor country. The local landowners had abused the peasantry for hundreds of years, and there had been uprisings before, but they had been no more than jacqueries, tinged by prelapsarian racial nostalgia and millenarian longing. But exasperation by itself does not lead to organised revolution, only to sporadic, anarchic and ultimately ineffective revolt, after which everything returns to normal, tenfold revenge having first been exacted, however hated the normality; something else, some added ingredient, is necessary for revolution to occur.

That something, in this case, was a professor – of philosophy. A previous government had taken it into its head to revive, or at least to stimulate, the local economy by resuscitation of a university that had existed briefly in the city in the seventeenth century. Little did it know – little could anyone have known – that by doing so it was sowing the wind and about to reap the whirlwind.

The professor of philosophy was the kind of man who, modest enough on the exterior, made no distinction between his own biography and world history. He was the illegitimate son of a wealthy man who brought him up identically with his legitimate offspring, except in one important respect: expectations of inheritance. Whereas the legitimate sons could expect a life of ease in whatever state of idleness they chose, he had had to make his own way without a penny to his name once his education was over. His access to luxury was cut off the moment he received his degree from the best university in the country. Studiously and academically inclined, he sought with great difficulty the funds necessary to continue his studies in philosophy, the focus of his mind. Spinoza was his special subject and while, as a consequence immersing himself in the deepest abstractions, he was humiliatingly obliged also to keep himself by casual work infinitely beneath his intellectual level. He believed himself to be exploited and quickly came to the conclusion that this was the fate also of the great majority of mankind. He conceived it his duty (and well within his capacity) to liberate it. While neither writing his thesis nor performing menial work, he read economics and attended the meetings of radical groupuscules, all of a similar tendency but squabbling among themselves on the finer points of doctrine.

His thesis written, defended, accepted and even commended, he searched for a teaching post in a university. These were few, of course, for the demand for philosophers in poor countries is less even than that in rich. He anticipated a lean period, but this time he was in luck: the newly resuscitated university in the poorest province's capital needed a professor of philosophy and no well-established person would leave his post for so uncertain a prospect, lacking in prestige and without certainty of continuation. He was the only candidate for the post with a doctorate and was duly appointed.

None of those who appointed him could have guessed the secret ambitions or burning resentments that he had taken good care to hide. Until then, he had seemed a meek and hesitant introvert, traits accounted for by his social origins, since illegitimacy still conferred an ineradicable stigma on those born into the country's Catholic upper-middle class.

His appointment to the chair was the liberation of his inner-megalomaniac. His kingdom was small at first, but at least he was the absolute monarch of it. His students were the sons (few daughters) of the surrounding farmers and peasants, the first generation to be educated beyond the age of ten or eleven. They were putty in his hands, disciples at his feet.

He communicated his resentment to them, his flaming hatred, of all that existed, but he communicated something more: a vision of a perfect future in which all of the present discontents had disappeared for ever. Hitherto having learned everything by rote, the minds of his listeners were not critical. A jar cannot be filled unless it is empty. They learned that the essential connecting link between the terrible present and the blissful, shining future was pitiless revolutionary violence for which, when they committed it, History and not they would be responsible. It was History, not they, who cut throats, burnt people alive, and threw the children of the oppressors down wells. They needed to feel no guilt about it.

The movement grew and spread, the professor went into

hiding and took a *nom de guerre*. His intellectual grandiosity grew to what would have been comic proportions had it not been taken so seriously by those who came under his influence, for whom the mere mention of his name was a mystical incantation. They soon discovered the joys of viciousness in a righteous cause, to say nothing of the Macbethian difficulties of going back on massacre once committed. And to inflict suffering on others for the good of the world is a pleasure that it is difficult to give up. It was a luxury for those who had no other luxuries.

The young men of the movement were conforming when they thought they were rebelling. They had been brought up to obedience to superstitions, and the obedience remained, but this time to the thoughts of the professor. Their former superstition led them only to inefficacious drunken ceremonies, half-pagan, half-Christian, but their new superstition led them to violence. The professor's unquestionable word, when followed, was the beginning of a new epoch for the world. Starting from this poorest province of a poor country, it would, by a process of historical inevitability, spread to the entire world and install perfect peace and justice forever. This they believed with the blindest of faith, admixed with the pleasures of revenge.

I was met in the old city, now sentried, sandbagged and barbed-wired, by a local journalist whose name I had been given and who in turn had been given my name. He was a few years older than I, and I could tell at once that he was impassioned by his work, that it acted on him like a stimulant drug. He lived and breathed to tell the world about the dangers of the movement, but the world outside his country hardly took notice. He told me within two minutes of meeting me the movement was within a hairsbreadth of taking over, and then the world would witness a massacre to dwarf all others (the Rwandan genocide had not yet taken place, but it would not have altered his opinion if it had, for the former professor had said that it would not matter if ninety per cent of the population disappeared so long as the remaining ten per cent was what he called 'pure,' ideologically without blemish). Furthermore, he told me, the revolution was for export and would soon engulf the neighbouring countries and the whole continent. By fearing, hating and exposing the movement's activities – to the maximum of his powers – he had made himself a marked man: but, like Luther, he could do no other. And I must admit that such was the force of his conviction that he communicated it to me, who already believed it though somewhat less passionately. A native of the place, he told me that when the movement had begun, some years before, no one had taken it seriously and it was almost a joke, at least from the intellectual point of view, though a murderous one from the outset. Its first public act was to hang a dog from a lamppost with a placard round it, a puzzling beginning whose Maoist allusion no one at first understood. But no one now mistook the deadly earnestness of its intentions. He had lived through its growth and could not readily believe that it would ever stop. He thought he had survived only because he was useful to the movement: his alarmist reports sowed panic and were thought to be demoralising. When panic and demoralisation were no longer useful to the movement, he would be the first to be killed.

The movement had just issued a proclamation that its final assault would begin in two days' time. It had issued such proclamations before and nothing had happened; but this, said my new companion, Gustavo, was part of its psychological warfare, its game of cat and mouse, with both the government and population. It was a game that it could not lose, for there was no counter to it.

Tension always rose in the days before its proclaimed final assault (no one doubted that one day there would be such an assault), and it fell once it had failed to materialise. But the tension never quite fell to the level it had been at before. Complete relaxation was impossible – the movement always produced a *coup de théâtre*, such as a bomb in the parliament a few days after the date of the announced final assault had passed – but vigilance is wearying and impossible to maintain at its peak. The dangerous and erroneous thought even fleetingly passed through my mind that it would be better for the movement to take over and get it all over with than for the country to continue to suffer these paroxysms of unbearable tension. I thought of the insurrection as if it were pneumonia in the days before antibiotic treatment, in which the patient had a crisis from which he either died or recovered completely. I foolishly wondered whether the movement's thirst for blood might not be slaked by the achievement of power.

Gustavo, whose moustache, I noticed, twitched like the long antennae of a nervous insect, laboured under no such illusions, not even fleetingly. Those who commit atrocity have to continue, for present atrocity is the only way in which they can convince themselves that past atrocity was justified; and since I was the only foreign journalist likely to visit the city for months to come, it was his patriotic duty to convince me that Armageddon was at hand so that I could spread the word.

How does something immaterial like tension make itself

almost as physical as fog? A silence reigned in the stone city, and such pedestrians as ventured out seemed to be scurrying like mice trying to regain their mouseholes. The soldiers behind their shelters of sandbags were both bored and agitated, and one would not have been surprised if one of them had suddenly opened up and fired at random in the street to relieve his own unbearable anxiety. We were waiting for the barbarians.

Gustavo took me in hand. Even now, a quarter of a century later, I can conjure up his passionate intensity – which in his case was not because he was among the worst of men, but because he was among the best. His movements were those of a clockwork that had been maximally wound up and then released.

'They know you are here, of course,' he told me. 'They have their spies and informers everywhere. Everyone is under observation all the time. They know why you are here and what you are doing because you are with me. You are probably more use to them alive than dead, but I cannot guarantee it. They might change their mind.'

It was frightening, of course, but also flattering in a way to be the object of so much attention, to be of such significance to strangers that my life might be worth weighing in the balance.

'They are looking at you even now,' said Gustavo.

'Would they know that I am hostile to them?' I asked.

'Of course. But that is not the question for them. They are as avid for publicity as any film star. They divide enemies, that is to say everyone who is not for them, into two categories: the dispensable and the useful. For the moment, you and I are useful, though that could change at any time. The moment I am no longer useful…' He made the universally understood gesture of having his throat cut.

'But how are you useful to them now?' I asked. 'Everything you write about them is extremely hostile.'

'I increase fear: that is what they want. But when I cease to do that, or when they no longer need people to be afraid that they will take power because they have taken power…' He did not need to explain further.

From then on, he acted as my guide, showing me what he thought I ought to see and witnessing what he thought I ought to witness. For example, he took me to the outskirts of the city, a little beyond its built-up area. There a large low building of mud stood in a field of dust. It was the military brothel. There was an orderly queue of enlisted men outside – the most orderly queue I had seen since my arrival in the country – as they waited their turn before entering and relieving themselves from the other tension that they suffered while waiting for the barbarians. Their encounters with whoever was inside were not of long duration: they emerged from the building still hitching up the trousers of their military fatigues. I never discovered how many women there were in the building, but it was all arranged like an efficient production line – I almost said like a military operation.

He also took me to ghost villages where the entire population had been massacred, supposedly for treachery or betrayal of 'the people', from whom they had excluded themselves by passing information on to the army, no doubt under threat from that quarter too. All that remained of the population were mounds in the earth signifying mass graves and a famished dog or two scavenging between the ruins. There were slogans that the massacrers had posted on the village walls after they had killed everyone: 'This is what happens to Enemies of the People' or 'Death to the running dogs of the bourgeoisie.'

Gustavo did not suppose that the army was composed of gentlemen who employed only the most scrupulous methods. A war like this – between a corrupt social order on the one hand and a movement of genocidal madmen on the other – was not a sporting competition with fixed rules and a referee to arbitrate them. The army's main instruments in its efforts to win the hearts and minds of the peasantry were the abduction, disappearance and presumed disposal of those deemed sympathetic to, or to have helped, the movement, even if it were only under duress. As one might have expected, standards of proof were low: rumours and whispers were more than sufficient, and land or other disputes between peasants were often solved by means of denunciation to the army. Everyone was afraid of everyone.

In response to criticisms from abroad by pressure groups that sought to protect the poor from violations by the government, an army commission had been set up to investigate allegations against the army itself of abductions and disappearance: but not only was this commission unable to discover what had happened to anyone, but it led to a new wave of abduction and disappearances of those associated with anyone who complained to it. Gustavo took me to interview two peasants, man and wife, who had naively gone to the commission to enquire of their son who had been removed from their home by four men in fatigues and balaclavas whom they presumed to be soldiers. They, the parents, had then fled for safety to the town from their village after having made their enquiries. There they hoped to be able to dissolve inconspicuously in the crowd, for they were now the enemies both of the army for having complained about it, their enquiry implying that they believed that the army carried out such abductions, and of the movement for having gone to its commission in the first place because it implied a belief in the possible honesty or trustworthiness of the army and therefore in the legitimacy of the bourgeois order. The other villagers shunned them as troublemakers and wanted not to be seen to be associated with them in any way, neither by the army nor the movement. They now lived in a hovel of corrugated iron and polythene on the edge of the city where they shared a room, divided in two by a sheet that served as a partition, with another family that had fled a village, though they did not know the reasons they had done so. Gustavo arranged our meeting in the cathedral, almost the only place where we could not be overheard. We spoke as we kneeled as if in prayer, at a distance from the few other believers who came to pray at that hour. Of course, the movement intended to do away with religion as a mere veil that hid their oppression from the oppressed.

I had been in the city for three days (it seemed much longer, for intensity of impressions can drive away memory of previous existence and make it appear that one has always lived in the present circumstances) when Gustavo came to me while I was eating my breakfast. Perhaps it is a sign of strength of character, or alternatively of a deep insensitivity, that no circumstances in which I have found myself, and nothing I have ever witnessed, has ever affected my appetite. I was therefore enjoying myself when Gustavo appeared. He was evidently in a state of great excitement.

'Come with me!' he said. 'Straight away! Bring your

camera.'

I did as I was told and (with regret) abandoned my breakfast. We walked through the streets too breathless for him to explain to me why we were doing so or whither we were going. We left the small colonial heart of the city, with its grand and simple stone buildings, austere but at the same time luxurious, and reached the more modern but higgledy-piggledy outskirt, ugly beyond description, everything built or merely constructed with no thought except tomorrow's immediate utility, and festooned with all the insignia of a desperate and impoverished commercialism. Our destination, it turned out, was the city morgue.

We arrived just in time to witness a small procession of peasants arriving from an outlying village, bearing two stretchers. Gustavo called on the procession to halt and it did so as if he were possessed of some official authority. The peasants were so cowed by life, perhaps, that they would have obeyed anyone who gave them orders with an air of confidence.

On each of the two stretchers was a body, not long dead. Judging by their clothes, they were a man and a woman, but it was their faces that I shall always remember. I had travelled the world and seen many terrible or tragic things – a mother and her six dead children laid out in descending size like organ pipes on the ground in Africa, seemingly perfectly preserved, after they had been crushed and suffocated by the sacks of maize on which they had been riding on a truck that had failed to make it up a steep hill, the mother and children sliding off first followed by the sacks on top of them – but I had never seen anything remotely to equal this.

Their faces had been flayed as illustrated in old anatomical plates, the skin carefully and even skilfully removed, to reveal the livid musculature below. Their eyes stared out in sightless horror, their teeth appearing between the slightly parted lips. It was so horrifying that for a time one's mind immediately emptied of all thought, one's body lost all power of action.

The mind cannot remain a vacuum for very long, however, and the most disturbing questions rose to it. Were the couple still alive when this was done to them, did one of them observe the other being tortured in this way? Were they killed first, and if so how (no other injury being visible on them)?

The stretcher-bearers put down their loads on the ground. They had borne them several miles and were obviously exhausted in more ways than one. A crowd gathered round the stretchers like vultures. I felt rather like one myself.

Gustavo told me what had happened. How he knew I do not know, but I suppose a kind of bush telegraph was in operation. The victims were the *alcalde*, or village mayor, and his wife. The movement had previously warned candidates for elections for any position whatever, from village mayor to president of the republic, that they would be subject to what it called 'revolutionary justice' if they continued to seek election. Where it couldn't actually prevent elections, it would punish the victors as complicit in the anti-people regime, which was both unambiguously imperialist and cravenly comprador.

The previous mayor had also been killed, though by having his throat slashed across with a machete. Whether from ambition – the *alcalde* was a position from which it was possible in a small way to extort money from the other villagers – or from conviction that it was his civic duty not to succumb to pressure and to resist the movement's drive to power, the mayor had participated in the election for the old mayor's successor. He was therefore especially to be made an example of for so foolhardily having thumbed his nose at the movement. He had been in the post only three weeks when he and his wife met their fate. Unlike the justice of the state in which cases often remained undecided for many years to the corrupt benefit of an army of lawyers, revolutionary justice was swift and decisive, with no appeal. There was no doubt that it was exemplary too: no other villager would come forward to take the mayor's place.

I had taken my fill of this terrible sight and made a movement to withdraw from it, but Gustavo, agitated, urged me to take photographs of it first. At first I protested that it would be an intrusion, an act of ghoulishness to do so, but he countered that the world should know, be visually informed, of what was going on in his country. In fact, it was my actual duty to take photographs; not to do so would be a failure to do it, false delicacy, cowardice.

Was he right? Perhaps, if I used the photographs for the uses he suggested: and he reiterated his previous arguments that at least the world would not be able to say afterwards that it had not been warned, etc. but still the horror of the scene paralysed my will.

'It's vital,' said Gustavo. 'You will be doing an immense service to my country.'

A foolish and unworthy thought occurred to me: perhaps he had arranged the whole *mise-en-scène* for me. Then I felt a slight pressure on my back as he pushed me forward with my camera.

I felt decidedly awkward. How would the peasants who had brought the bodies react to my intrusion? Would they see it as callous, an act of voyeuristic tourism, making a spectacle of their situation? Might they turn angry?

My paralysis was over. I decided to take the photographs and thus rid myself of my previous unworthy thoughts about Gustavo. Something strange then happened to me. I lost sight of the horror before me, and began to think only of the light, the background, the angle, the composition of the pictures I took. I worried no longer what the villagers or other spectators might think: my problem had become to take the best pictures possible, for I knew that the newspapers back home would demand high quality. I circled the stretchers on the ground as a vulture hops round a piece of carrion, wondering where best to start to peck at it. And the click of my camera now sounded as loud to me as a clap of thunder.

I felt an exaltation, a self-importance as I took my pictures. I was doing the world's work; nothing in the world was more important than what I was doing. If I did nothing else in my life, these pictures would have justified my existence. I would have gained a small immortality.

This was in the days before digital cameras and my film ran out. I had no other film with me and had only to hope that the pictures I had taken would come out well. I signalled to Gustavo that I had finished, and we left the scene. I now considered my photographs so important that I could think of nothing except getting them home for publication (in those days, electronic transmission was hardly possible). I was gripped by a kind of fever.

I returned to the capital by a military flight that Gustavo arranged for me. We embraced and swore eternal friendship as I departed from the military airfield, but I knew from experience that such brief and intense encounters seldom, if ever, gave rise to lasting friendships: but of course we fully meant what we said at the time.

When I arrived once again in the capital I discovered to my chagrin and intense frustration that it was impossible to arrange an immediate flight home, that I would have to stay for several days. The bourgeoisie were fleeing the country, it seemed, and all the flights to Miami, my way-station home, were fully booked. I would have to kick my heels for a time in the capital.

What could I do there? Never having been one to tolerate complete inactivity, and always having found in prisons a subject of great interest, I decided to visit my compatriots (of whom I learned there were two) in the capital's notorious penitentiary. They were there for drug-smuggling, of course, the country being one of the largest producers and exporters of cocaine. The movement, it was said, had taken to 'protecting' the peasant growers of the plant, as well as the small processors of its leaf, from the corrupt depredations of the state, in return for revolutionary 'taxes'. It was a bargain the peasants and processors could not very well refuse; and the movement believed that by its protection racket it was not only serving the economic interests of the country but promoting the downfall of world imperialism by undermining the moral and physical fibre of imperialist countries' populations, softening them up for their eventually inevitable defeat. A people concerned exclusively with its solipsistic pleasures would not be in a position to resist an onslaught by a disciplined alliance of the world's workers and peasants. Not, of course, that the money the movement obtained in the meantime was unwelcome: its expenses were considerable, because it had to buy its more sophisticated arms from the army, whose generals sold them dear.

The prison was a vast one, at least in number of inmates, of whom there were several thousand. Until a few months previous there had been even more, for it had been the main holding centre for captured guerrillas, or those at least accused of having been such. There were undoubtedly true believers among them, missionaries so to speak, who had been moulded and formed in the professor's university who took complete control of captives. These prisoners occupied a separate building, even more grossly overcrowded than the others, where they lived not in the anarchy that reigned elsewhere in the prison but under the iron discipline of the fanatical revolutionary hierarchy. They held military drills and the government feared that they might one day break out and seed themselves through the capital, already rotted enough by their coreligionists. Then, two months before, they had risen in revolt against the conditions in which they were held, demanding special privileges as prisoners of war. There was only one way of dealing with the problem and one thing to do: to send in the army with bazookas and flame-throwers. All fourteen hundred of the movement's prisoners were crushed or burned to death, the evidence being swiftly removed by truck and bulldozer, to the great consternation of what counts as the world, at least until something else happened to occupy its mind. But the government learnt its lesson and now took no prisoners, killing them wherever they were taken, in piecemeal and dispersed fashion, and therefore less visibly to the rest of the world.

The embassy gave me the names of the two British prisoners – a third had died of appendicitis the week before, or so the prison authorities claimed – and told me that no special permission was necessary for me to visit them. All I needed to do – this struck me as strangely casual in a country in such a state of crisis, laxity being tempered by murder - was to present myself with my passport at the prison gate, along with all the other visitors, at the appropriate time. Once inside the prison, I would easily find someone to direct or take me to the British prisoners.

I followed the advice closely and it turned out to be good, at least from the point of view of securing my ends. I went to the prison in a taxi, asking the driver to drop me off at a little distance from the gate. I suspected that it would not do to be seen by the other visitors to arrive by that means.

I needn't have worried, of course. In front of the prison was a huge open space, waste ground in effect, and it was there that more than a thousand visitors waited for admission. They were, for such a large crowd, surprisingly orderly, having organised themselves in a snake-like queue, the most, indeed only the second, orderly crowd I had seen since my arrival in the country. Perhaps the guards, who patrolled the line with leashed Alsatians, ensured the order.

The visitors, as was only to be expected, were (as everywhere else) in overwhelming majority women. They were also overwhelmingly mestiza, of mixed racial descent. Two decades before, the prison had been situated in bleak and arid semi-desert, but now the city had caught up with it and – apart from this waste ground set aside for the purpose – it was surrounded by habitations of breezeblock and tin, mud and polythene that had grown up uncontrollably with the flight from the countryside. Overhead was a tangle of wires, like the web of a spider after having been exposed to cannabis, that brought electricity, and sometimes electrocution, to the residents. Water was brought to them by ancient fuel tankers, so worn down by work that they progressed by little jerks, as if they were just about to expire.

Up and down the lines of visitors, steering well clear of the guards, peasant women offered roasted maize for their sustenance. There were traders too in sweet bottled drinks, biscuits, chewing gum, cigarettes sold by the unit, and that eternal standby of impoverished street hawkers, shoelaces.

In front and behind me were two women whose age I found it hard to estimate. We started to talk, and they told me that their husbands whom they were visiting had been held in the prison for three and four years respectively without trial so far, and they had forgotten, if they had ever known, what it was that they were alleged to have done. They said all this without any of the querulous resentment of the rightly accused, outraged by the justice of an accusation. They seemed neither surprised nor embittered by the false imprisonment of their menfolk, for injustice here was like the weather, against whose vagaries it was pointless to complain. They could not afford lawyers though this was a land of lawyers, many of whom were without sufficient employment to keep them in the middle class.

Suddenly there was a strange movement in the lines of visitors, like a ripple caused by a gust of wind in a surface of calm water, or a herd of grazing animals suddenly aware of the approach of a predator. At a distance I saw that some guards in green uniforms had suddenly emerged from the main entrance of the prison swinging long flexible rubber truncheons above their head: they laid about the visitors nearest to them. I was too far away from them to discern any possible reason for their attack, if there had been one: perhaps it was simply a demonstration of arbitrary power exercised to instil a proper respect. The chastisement over, the guards withdrew into the prison as suddenly as they had emerged from it. I asked the two women whether they had any idea of the reason for this demonstration of force, but they were unable to tell me, except that this often happened. The visitors seldom escaped entirely unscathed.

Then we, the visitors, our powerlessness having been successfully demonstrated, were let into the prison. We moved forward slowly but the search once inside the gates was perfunctory and consisted largely of handing over bribes to the guards in the form of a proportion of whatever the visitors had brought with them as presents for the prisoners they were visiting. This was all quite open and unabashed; from me, the guard who searched me took a few dollars before giving me a token with a number on it which he entered in a book against my name, warning me that the token had to be presented as a condition of leaving the prison. Loss of the token would result in incarceration (women who lost their tokens being removed to the women's prison elsewhere). The whole system was open to abuse, of course, which perhaps was its purpose. Some of the few male visitors were professional replacers of prisoners: for a fee, they agreed to take a prisoner's place for a time. This transaction, alone of all transactions in the prison, was based on trust: trust that the prisoner who thus obtained his temporary release would return on the agreed date. The guards, of course, connived at the deception, but had to share their takings with those above them in the hierarchy.

Once inside the prison, there was a milling crowd of prisoners waiting for their visitors. No one was waiting for me, of course, but a prisoner with an insinuating manner spotted me at once as an economic opportunity and attached himself to me, having offered in return for five dollars to take me to the cell of whomever I had come to see. A professional.

He knew the British prisoners. This was hardly surprising: Europeans must have been very conspicuous in that pullulating world. He would take me straight to them, he said, and protect me both on the way and throughout my time in the prison.

There were many prison blocks, arranged in ranks like the public housing scheme of slum-clearance. They looked as if they had been built with easy destruction by artillery in mind, for their shabbily constructed walls were of breezeblock held together by poor-quality mortar. Perhaps the authorities had not wanted them to be convertible into impregnable fortresses; perhaps it was merely that whoever had built them had cheated on the contract.

As my guide – Eduardo, he said he was called, though whether or not this was really his name I could not say – and I walked through the prison, I received some discomfiting and no doubt appraising stares. Some of them were distinctly predatory. Eduardo warned me to stick closely to him: it had not been unknown for visitors such as I to be kidnaped and ransomed. I am not a nervous man but I at once began to imagine an ambush at every step. A man is never very far removed from paranoia.

This was a world suffused with greyness. The ground was grey, the buildings were grey, the sky was grey. It was like being in a black and white film, the celluloid of which had faded.

The prisoners wore no uniforms but ragged casual clothes of the type that most people in the world now wear most of the time. Holes were conspicuous, as were those few garments that were well-laundered. There were social distinctions even here, and the manner of the prisoners varied too: from the preening cock-of-the-walk to the furtive slink of attempted invisibility.

We entered one of the blocks and climbed a rough and collapsible, if not actually collapsing, stairway to the top floor, five floors up. There was a constant to-and-from on the stairway, and I quickly came to the conclusion that it was better to catch no one's eye but avert one's gaze from any appraising stare. It was a fine line to tread between cowering and offering a challenge, and I began to regret my imprudence in having come. The dye, however, was cast.

There was more space, it was less crowded, on the top floor. It was relatively quiet with less of a constant hubbub punctuated by angry shouting. The noise below had been like a continuous blow on the face. My frantic desire to escape it would very soon have dissolved any scruple in doing whatever was necessary to escape it. One accommodates to smell, but not to noise. I had noticed that there were no warders anywhere: the prison appeared to be internally self-governing.

We approached a cell. It was where one of the British prisoners… lived? lodged? was confined? What was the right word to describe it? Did it matter? Does our world make our words, or our words make our world? It is strange how philosophical questions rise unbidden in the mind at the most inappropriate moments, as mice wash their paws when cornered by a cat.

Outside the cell, sitting in a stool, was a large, unwashed man, tough-looking rather than athletic, a mestizo with black stubble on his chin that added to the ferocity of his appearance. His facial expression was one of concentrated malignity. His profession – protection – was his pleasure.

'His bodyguard,' whispered Eduardo, who then spoke to him in argot that I could not understand.

The man's teeth glinted with gold dentistry. This was both a reward for and sign of successful past violence. Decay usually takes teeth from the rear, violence from the front. Gold repair, or mere decoration, requires funds, raised by such a man in only one way. Gold dentistry were as much a warning in this man as bright colours in poisonous frogs.

After a brief exchange, the bodyguard entered the cell, having first banged on its rusting iron door. He might have been able to pick you up, smash you against the wall and land punches in your stomach, but he was still a servant. I noticed that the cell door required no unlocking.

The bodyguard soon reappeared. He nodded to me to enter by inclining his head in the direction of the cell. He looked at me now with less suspicion, almost with respect.

I entered the cell alone, leaving Eduardo to whatever conversation he might have with the bodyguard. It was, of course, a small chamber, no more than eight feet by ten, but it was surprisingly homely, almost snug. The walls were hung with pictures, of landscapes rather than of the expected nudes, and over the iron bed was thrown a woven textile rug of the kind that Indian women had tried to sell tourists in the days when there were tourists. At the other end of the cell, sitting on a plain deal chair, was the prisoner. He stood and came forward to greet me. I felt like Stanley meeting Livingstone.

He was of middling height and slight of build, reduced yet further, I should say, by illness. He was older than I had expected, or at least had aged. He was in his late thirties, and some grey was beginning to show in his lank brown hair. His eyes were bright and alert. He held out his somewhat bony hand for me to shake, and we exchanged the time of day in a surprisingly formal manner.

There followed an awkward silence between us.

'To what do I owe...?' he then asked.

His accent revealed that he was from the North of England, and his manner of speaking from the middle class. And if he were not educated, it was certainly not from lack of intelligence.

Oddly enough, I had not thought in advance of how I should explain my presence in the prison. Much in my life seemed undertaken almost at random, or on a very slight pretext. Why had I come? Curiosity? Prurience? I had not thought to bring anything – books, for example – to the prisoners.

'I'm a doctor,' I said. 'I have an interest in prison conditions around the world.'

That much was true – to an extent, for my interest was casual and to no serious end, such as combatting tuberculosis in them would have been. Come to think of it, the prisoner could have been suffering from that disease, so cachectic was he. His chest was hollow, his cheeks concave. I think he sensed that he was for me an object of idle enquiry, a trophy or exhibit in my mental cabinet of curiosities. Still, he was soon friendly enough, for I was, I subsequently discovered, the first of his compatriots to visit him in a long time, other than the consul on his annual perfunctory visit to the prison, where he made clear that he thought that the prisoners had made their own bed and now should lie on it. In such circumstances, one becomes friendly even with those one has no reason to trust.

Having introduced ourselves – he was Robert – I asked a natural question: how long had he been here?

Six years, he said, nine more to do.

'Drug smuggling, I suppose?' I asked.

'Of course. That's what all the foreign prisoners are in for.'

He made no pretence or protestations of innocence, of not having done what he was accused of having done. He and his friend had been back-packing for two years through South America for reasons as idle as mine in visiting him (idlers understand each other's lack of motive) when they ran out of funds. They now wanted to return home, preferably with a little money in their pockets, but they hadn't enough even for the fare, their families refusing any longer to support them. The solution was obvious: and soon enough they met someone in a bar, a low dive, who offered them the opportunity to carry cocaine. The profit that was held up before them like a mirage in the desert would have been sufficient to have seen them right for a time.

It had almost worked. They appeared to have survived the checks at the airport and were sitting in celebratory mood, congratulating themselves on their cool cleverness in the aircraft that was soon (they thought) to take off. The engines were about to start up but then the craft was boarded at the last moment by five policemen, indistinguishable from soldiers, one of them obviously the superior officer of the others. They walked up and down the aisle staring hard at the passengers. They knew who they were looking for all along, of course: they just wanted to heighten the tension so that the arrest came almost as a relief and their victims willing to give themselves up into their custody.

They seized the two smugglers and dragged them from the plane. There would have been no point in resistance, even if they had been innocent. The other passengers would not have come to their assistance even had they been nuns; but their appearance was against them. They had tried to make themselves look respectable, but it was too obviously a deliberate attempt to be convincing after years of tramping with no money, the consumption of various drugs, and several bouts of dysentery. They were obvious suspects.

The passengers looked at them as they were hauled away with faces that varied from hostility to complacency, passing through disdain. Some were angered, no doubt, by the delay to the take-off; others, perhaps, enjoyed the drama and their hearts were secretly warmed by imagining the long punishment of the guilty. But once the policemen had dragged the two of them away from the appraising eyes of witnesses, they felt free to subject them to a little mistreatment; twisting their arms and necks, punching them in the stomach, and so forth. There was nothing personal in this except, perhaps, an additional pleasure in mistreating gringos: it was, otherwise, part of normal procedure. It was a foretaste of what was to come if they did not cooperate.

In any case, it would have been difficult to deny all knowledge of the twelve kilos of cocaine in their luggage wrapped in their exiguous personal effects. A smaller quantity might have been insinuated into their luggage, but not so large a proportion of the whole. They were promised a short sentence against a swift admission of guilt, five years maximum against a potential of thirty, and the consul of the time had been neither helpful nor sympathetic to their plight: he was tired of having to deal with ne'er-do-wells just because they happened to be his compatriots. It was his job, of course, but we do not all like our jobs or do them with enthusiasm.

'I don't suppose the policemen who found the cocaine

destroyed it,' I said.

'Ha!' exclaimed Robert. 'This country exists on cocaine, from top to bottom. Everything you eat, everything you drink, everything you do or buy is paid for with cocaine.'

An exaggeration, of course, but the kind a journalist might make to grab the attention of his reader. It was not as if the country had been an economic *tabula rasa* until there was cocaine or would simply starve to death without it. But I knew what Robert meant.

'We were double-crossed,' resumed Robert. 'They gave us fifteen instead of five. The reason was obvious.'

'What was it?' I asked.

'With a long sentence like that, we would be more desperate to bribe them.'

'You might have been caught at the other end,' I said.

'They don't catch more than five or ten per cent,' said Robert. 'We thought the odds were good, it was a risk worth taking. It was the only way we could make twenty thousand in a short time.'

'What would you have done with it?'

'Look,' continued Robert, ignoring my question, and replying as if I had accused him of something, 'it wasn't our fault if people wanted to snort cocaine. If there's a demand, there'll be a supply. If we hadn't done it, someone else would. You won't stop a message getting through by shooting the messenger.'

'How will you stop it, then? And ought it to be stopped?'

It was curious how quickly we had slid from personal experience to abstractions, such as the ethics of drug-taking and smuggling. Men are like that, but not women.

'Have you seen how the peasants live on the sierra?' asked

Robert. He was now implicitly posing as some kind of humanitarian, or at least as a person deeply concerned for others. 'They have an incredibly hard life. For them, growing cocaine is a heaven-sent opportunity. They get three crops a year, the plant has no diseases or pests and doesn't need looking after, and its price is ten times at least what they can get for growing anything else, even if they get only a hundredth of its eventual value. Can you blame them for growing it? And then the government comes along, under the pressure from the Yanks, and sprays their fields from aeroplanes to kill the bushes so that they can grow a bit of corn or a few potatoes once the effect of the herbicide has worn off. Are you surprised, then, that the peasants in the sierra support the movement?'

This made some sense, of course, even if the revolutionary movement extracted payment from them and its ultimate goal was the abolition of money. You couldn't expect the peasants to know that: what they saw was the guerrillas trying to shoot down the crop-sprayers. As for the profits made by the dealers, they were no more known to the peasants than were the debates in the national congress. The ultimate goal of the movement, a world revolution such that demand for cocaine would wither away like the state, was so abstract that it meant nothing to the peasants. Those who know the struggle to eat more than once a day do not concern themselves much with distant prospects. All this, as Robert explained it, was meant as a self-justification and therefore as an implicit protest against the injustice that he and his companion had suffered.

'So those who take cocaine back home are rendering a service to the peasants of this country, or at least to those who live in the cocaine-cultivating areas?'

'What right,' replied Robert, 'has any government to tell me or anyone else what we can take and what we can't? It's my body, after all, and I can do what I like with it.'

'But when things go wrong,' I asked, 'who is to pay for it?' And then I asked a more interesting question. 'By the way, do you take it?'

'No,' he said, 'not any more.'

'Why not?'

'I saw what it did to people. It sent them mad, it gave them heart attacks, it destroyed their noses – and their lives.'

Now he spent most of his time in the study of philosophy. His search for the grounds of existence seemed entirely disinterested: there was no object in it other than knowledge of the truth. It was relatively easy for him to obtain the books he needed, for they were not of a kind that anyone wished to steal even in this little world in which every other material object had to be carefully guarded and had its price. There were two books, I noticed, on his table: Wittgenstein's *Tractatus* and MacIntyre's *After Virtue*, both of them well-thumbed. (When a man reads at all, it is well to know *what* he reads, if you want to know him.) These were not beginners' books in philosophy and suggested that he had engaged on his search for some time. Whether he would find what had so far eluded Mankind for millennia was doubtful: but no search was better suited to a long term of imprisonment than that for something that could not be found.

'Would you like to see round the prison?' asked Robert.

'Very much,' I replied.

He squeezed past me and rapped on the cell door. The huge man outside opened it.

'Si, señor,' he said deferentially.

The politeness of his address surprised me. He could easily have broken Robert's arm like a matchstick. Even in this environment, brute force did not entirely reign. It was money and the ability to pay that counted, and in the kingdom of the destitute, the man with a penny reigns.

Robert told him that we were going for a little walk, and he needed no extra instruction to tell him to stick close behind us. That was his job, and I noticed that his eyes swivelled continuously, almost like those of a chameleon, surveying the limited horizon for the approach of possible attackers. Certainly, he looked intimidating enough, but the fear of the need for such protection outweighed in my mind the reassurance of its provision.

'We'll descend to hell first,' said Robert.

Hell was the floor on which the prisoners with no means to pay for anything lived. They had to subsist on such largesse as the government offered them, supplemented by theft and any scraps they could obtain by force, fraud or begging. Their clothes were rags, they slept communally on the concrete floor without anything to cushion them in their slumbers, they lived like maggots in an angler's tin, constantly jostling for space. Silence and privacy were unknown to them, though whether they had never experienced them and therefore did not miss them I was unable to ascertain. They looked on our visit with no particular favour, as if Robert were a member of an upper class slumming it for his own amusement.

In the corner of the comfortless, bare and unadorned hall in which so many human souls lived and breathed and took their being was a huge black cauldron with a charcoal fire beneath. It might easily have taken ten men inside it and looked like a vessel inspired by the paintings of Bosch or Breughel to depict an inferno. Indeed, there was a rumour that a man had once been thrown in it, to teach him a lesson he would never forget – or remember. The meal that day had some substance to it.

By the cauldron stood two sweaty cooks, if cooks they could be called, who from time to time mounted wooden pedestals and plunged great wooden sticks to stir whatever the cauldron contained, some kind of maize porridge. Around the rim and down the sides of the cauldron towards its top was a thick crust of dried porridge, the accretion I should imagine of weeks if not of years. When the cooks saw us, they gave us a malevolent grin, as if we were somehow observing our own future. One of them seemed to wink.

'That's what you get if you can't afford anything else,' said Robert.

There was some kind of eruption within the cauldron, like a bubble bursting in molten lava, that emitted a foul stench. Sulphur would almost have been better.

'Let's ascend the social scale,' said Robert when he saw, not without amusement, that I had had enough.

As we climbed the stairs again, his bodyguard still glued to us, Robert explained that here, as everywhere else, you lived according to your means. The higher the floor of your cell, the less crowded they were and the higher your status. You paid rent for your cell to the prison authorities, illegally of course, who kept it in proportion to their grade. Non-payment of rent was immediately followed by eviction back to the lowest level from which we had just come. To evict a prisoner from a cell was almost the only purpose for which the warders entered the blocks, always in military-strength force. On the top floor there were cells that had been knocked into luxury apartments, opulently furnished with all possible conveniences. Prostitutes were on call for those who could afford them, and food and drink brought in from outside at any time of the day or night.

'Of course,' said Robert, 'there are drawbacks and disadvantages to living up here.'

'Drawbacks?'

'As you go higher, there are fewer prisoners on each floor. It's a social pyramid. Everyone hates or envies the people on the floor above him. You must have noticed that every door has a guard outside.'

'Come to think of it, yes.'

'How do you think order is kept here?'

I pointed to Robert's bodyguard, who had kept only a pace behind us throughout. I had the impression that Robert regarded him very much as he might have regarded a guard dog.

'No,' he said, 'he's just my personal protection that I need for special reasons that I'll tell you about. No, on the upper floors we pay for protection as part of our rent. It's subcontracted by the guards to an outside gang. If there's any trouble, they come in and start shooting, no questions asked. They know that down below.'

'Has it ever happened?'

'A couple of years ago. The floor below organised a raid on us. The gang came in and started shooting. Fifteen were killed, including three of us. Besides, while they were raiding, the floor below *them* tried to raid their floor and they had to retreat. They haven't tried anything since.'

'So there's a kind of law and order?'

'You could call it that, I suppose. It's like any law and order: it's the rule of the strongest, which means the richest.'

We were back on his floor, the fifth. Already it felt like home. Noise, like heat, rises, but it abates on the way. It was almost like calm.

'Shall we go up on the roof?' asked Robert.

We climbed a narrow spiral staircase and emerged through a trap-door on to a flat roof. I felt like Christ being shown the world by the Devil: except, of course, that Robert was able to offer me nothing except words and I was no Christ.

We were alone on the roof. By now I had learned to discount the bodyguard as one forgets air until one can't breathe.

'Why is there no one else here?' I asked. You would have thought that the chance of isolation would have appealed to at least some prisoners.

'It's forbidden and the guards have orders to shoot on sight,' replied Robert. 'They think the roof is where riots start. Of course, they're very bad shots and there's usually time to get down before they bring out the machine guns. Even they can't miss with those.'

Were we being aimed at even as we spoke?

'But that's not the main reason,' continued Robert.

'What's the main reason?'

'If you're up on the roof you can be thrown off, if you have enemies. And everyone has enemies.'

It was true that there was nothing between the edge of the roof and the ground below, not even a low parapet.

'Take a look,' said Robert.

I approached the edge gingerly, following him. My desire to show no fear was greater than my desire to preserve my life.

'Look!' he said, pointing to another part of the prison next to this block, a prison within a prison as it were. It had a high concrete wall around it, surmounted by metal spikes and formidable rolls of barbed wire.

'That's where the dangerous prisoners are kept,' he said.

The dangerous prisoners! What could they have been like? I was soon to see.

'The guards never go in there,' said Robert, 'except with an armed escort. Then they shoot their way in.'

Against the inside of one of the walls was an array of open latrines. Between them and the prison building was another wall like a screen that I imagine was supposed to provide some slight privacy. Even from our vantage point, we could detect the mephitic odours of unemptied cesspits.

A man came to relieve himself on one of the latrines. He looked around furtively, not from modesty but from fear. It was justified.

Another prisoner, who had obviously followed him, had stealthily scaled the low wall. He had a large quadripartite fishing hook, of the kind used to catch sharks, with him. Suddenly he unleashed it, swinging it like a lasso, at the man relieving himself. He missed his aim, but only very narrowly, and prepared for a second attempt. His intended victim pulled up his trousers as swiftly as possible and fled.

Despite myself, I felt my legs tremble. I had been on the roof only a matter of seconds and I had already witnessed an attempted murder, or at least an attempt to maim another human being seriously. Seeing my reaction, Robert laughed.

'That's nothing,' he said. 'Sometimes there are five murders a week in there. It's the only way any of them leave. They throw the bodies over the wall for the guards to take them away. Sometimes they get caught in the barbed wire. They leave them for a few days. I suppose they think it's some kind of lesson. The men in white boiler suits and helmets come and disentangle them.'

I think Robert enjoyed telling his horror stories. The more terrifying the environment, the more admirable his survival. It established a type of superiority over me.

'Have you seen enough?' he asked.

I nodded, and we returned to the comparative safety of his cell. I sat on his chair, he on the bed. I opened the *Tractatus* and sought its famous last line: Whereof one cannot speak, thereof one must be silent.

'Philosophy!' exclaimed Robert. 'With it, I could be enclosed in a nutshell and count myself king of infinite space.' Then he added, as if to forestall any accusation of pretension, 'We did *Hamlet* at school.'

From this I concluded what I had in any case suspected, that he had not been a dunce at school – they don't teach *Hamlet* to dunces – and further that he had not adopted his mode of life from a lack of prospects. He had been a victim, if he had been a victim at all, of the romantic rebellion that was considered at the time of his youth to be the only authentic way of behaving, of being a true human being rather than a mere cipher, conformity (except to rebellion) being indistinguishable from slavery.

'You were going to tell my why you need a personal bodyguard,' I said.

'It's a long story,' he replied.

'I have the time.' Visiting time at the prison ended at dusk.

'Well,' Robert began, 'we were friends, my co-accused and I. In fact, we were best friends, ever since school. We did everything together, we were inseparable. We travelled the world together. We crossed Africa and Asia.'

'In search of what?'

I had met such travellers in the course of my own travels. They started out on some vague quest, or with an unformed sense of curiosity, but after a few months or perhaps a year continued only because they could not think of anything else to do. Often their minds had been emptied of content because they had smoked too much dope. Their pride was in living as cheaply as possible, which for them was a sign of their virtuous rejection of consumer society and its shallowness. It never occurred to them that they were nevertheless living as parasites, as most of them still had small subventions from home without which they could not have survived. They were not without competitiveness, for when they met, they played a game of more-remote-than-thou: they had been to places more cut off from civilisation, or the rest of the world, than anyone else.

'After three years we had had enough, as I told you, but we had no money to go home. Our parents couldn't send us any more money. We were still friends at that stage, after three years and all we had gone through together. We'd been through a lot, had many scrapes and brushes with death.'

'Disease?'

'Among other things. Malaria, hepatitis, everyone gets it. Bandits a few times, not always where you'd expect them.' He paused. 'Would you like something to drink? I've got some good moonshine here, perfectly safe.'

'No thank you.'

'As you like. When we were arrested,' he resumed, 'this colonel came to us and offered to have us released us for forty thousand dollars each. He didn't believe at first that we hadn't got it or couldn't find it, he seemed to think that every foreigner had that kind of money. Then he dropped the price to twenty-five thousand each. That was his last offer, he said. We couldn't have raised twenty-five dollars, let alone twenty-five thousand. Our parents were tired of sending us money and told us we had made our bed etcetera. We'd lost contact with our friends in England. We were stuck.'

'What happened then?'

'We got used to the idea that this was where we were going to spend the next fifteen years of our lives. We had hoped the government would grow tired of paying for us and just deport us, but a prisoner doesn't cost much to keep here and anyway it probably just forgot about us.'

'And the British consul?'

'Useless. I've seen them come and go. All they're worried about is their next posting and their pension. They think we got what we asked for. They think they've been sent here just to go to cocktail parties.'

If I had been consul, I thought, I would have done just the same. I easily slip into conventional ways of thinking and conducting myself. And it was true that the prisoners were the kind of people – wasters – who brooked no interference with the way in which they chose to live, and then expected maximum assistance when things went wrong. Freedom from consequences is the most precious freedom of all, the acme of liberty.

'We had to learn how things worked in prison,' said Robert. 'The first thing that happened was that we were beaten up in a kind of welcome ceremony. They thought that because we were foreign drug-smugglers we must have money. They couldn't believe we had been caught first time, that we weren't regulars. We lived for a time in the hell down below. Eventually we got a message out to our parents – the consul passed it on, I'll say that for him. They got people together to pay for us to move up here. They're still paying.'

'Who are they paying?'

'The prison commandant. Of course, the minister takes his cut and there's a premium for foreigners. The present arrangement is to everyone's advantage.'

'So why the bodyguard?'

'I'm coming to that. After about a year we were still like blood brothers, my friend and I. Then we began to receive visits from an American pastor, First Church of Christ Redeemer, or something like that. He came, he said, to bring the Good News to prisoners. He held services for them.'

'The prisoners didn't look very religious to me,' I said.

'He didn't just preach, he arranged for little luxuries to be brought in, that he distributed to the sinners.'

'Like what?'

'Soap, shampoo. He must have bribed the authorities to let them in. only those who prayed with him got them, of course.'

'What was he like?'

'What did I think of him then, or what do I think of him now?'

'Then.'

'He was very friendly. He put his arm round you and squeezed. He was dressed in a very ordinary way: white shirt, artificial fibre trousers. He seemed never to have left the Mid-West. He knew that Jesus loved him and that Jesus would love everyone else too if they let him into their hearts.'

'Did he convert anyone?'

'Some pretended to be converted as long as the soap and shampoo kept coming.'

'What about you?'

'We never pretended but he kept coming to see us. We assumed that it was in the hope that one day we would convert. We would've been feathers in his cap.'

'But you didn't?'

'No. Then one day after about twelve weeks, he came to us with a proposition. By then we thought he was our friend. Why else would he have kept it up all this time? When you're stuck in here, you long for a friendly face from outside, especially if he speaks your language.'

'Like me,' I said, smiling.

'You're a bird of passage, a tourist. You'll never come again. I'll never see you again. That's why I can tell you all this. You can only trust people you don't know.'

It was true. I was a kind of voyeur without the power to do him harm.

'So you liked him?'

'Yes, how could we not? Of course, we knew that we wouldn't have chosen him as a friend if we hadn't been in here. He wasn't exactly our style, all that talk of sin and stuff, not that he tried it on very hard with us. But prisoners can't be choosers.'

'What did you talk about, then?'

'Everything. He brought us the news: in here, you get only rumour. Of course, there are some of the movement's plants in here, trying to recruit and spread rumours such as that the Movement is about to take over and set everyone in here free.'

'And do they believe it?'

'To begin with they did. There was a special kind of restlessness that ran through the prison.' He stopped to think of a simile. 'Like wind through the leaves of a tree...'

'Which soon dropped...' I said.

'The first time they announced the final assault, there was a complete silence in the prison. Then, as the day wore on and nothing happened, the whispering started and the agitation. They had expected to be free by the evening, but there was no sign of the supposed final assault. The government didn't want to admit even the possibility of a final assault because to have admitted it would have meant that they had lost control, so they allowed prison visiting as usual. On the other hand, the Movement told the people to stay indoors and not to go anywhere to demonstrate its support for the movement. So that day there weren't any visitors because the people feared the Movement more than they believed the government, except for a few who turned up at the prison gate who were deaf and dumb or for some reason didn't know what was going on. The guards thought they must have been terrorists and shot them dead.'

'A real propaganda coup.'

'For the Movement. Look how the regime treats the people, even the deaf and dumb! It's on its last gasp, it fears even the handicapped. It prefers to shoot the people rather than go quietly. But the time for revenge and punishment is near: that's what the Movement said.'

'What was the prisoners' attitude to the Movement?'

'Most prisoners don't think of anything except survival and getting out of here alive. Do you know the poem by Cavafy?'

'*Waiting for the Barbarians*?'

'Exactly. *Why are we gathered here and waiting in the marketplace? It is because of the barbarians, they will be here today.*'

'The poem ends, if I remember rightly, with the failure of the barbarians to arrive as expected.'

'*They were some kind of solution, the barbarians.* That's the last line.'

I love incongruity, and the incongruity of a discussion about the meaning of a poem by the fastidious Alexandrian Greek in such surroundings struck me forcefully, with a kind of joy, though also, at the same time, as almost natural: for what is literature for, if not to illuminate our lives in whatever situation we may find ourselves? Besides, many men begin to think only in extremity, as a last resort.

'The solution to what?' I asked.

'In a situation like this, your mind is freed.'

'From what?'

'The search for meaning. Here it is obvious.'

'And what is it?

'Survival.'

We had wandered far from the American pastor. I brought him back into the story.

'After a few months, he told us that he had contacts high up in the ministry that ran the prison. That seemed to be plausible because he had no difficulty in bringing his little bribes into the prison.'

'And then?'

'One day he told us he could get us released.'

'How?'

'By the usual method, bribes. He said he knew who to bribe and he could do it relatively cheaply.'

'A pastor acting as a conduit for bribes?'

'Render unto Caesar those things which are Caesar's.'

'And so?'

'He said he could get us out for twenty thousand each.'

'But that was still well beyond your means.'

'He said he knew how we could raise the money. He said he

had done it before, for prisoners in other South American countries.'

'How?'

'He said he would take pictures of our living conditions – actually of those on the ground floor, those in Hell – and send them home for publication in the local paper. He would write stories of how we had been ill-treated. He would give our parents ideas for raising the money locally and tell them that it was for a fine in place of prison, not a bribe. (He said that people wouldn't give money for a bribe, not even in a good cause.) To cut a long story short, our parents followed his advice and between them raised fifty thousand dollars in a few months for our release. It was the photographs that had shocked them.'

'They allowed him to take photographs?'

'I think he just had some pictures which he used for every case.'

'And what happened next?'

'They sent him the money.'

'And?'

'That was the last we saw of him. He probably fucked off to the next country, to do it all over again. He was a professional.'

A curious profession, though, acting as a pastor to find western prisoners in Third World gaols, gaining their trust, and running off with their money supposedly for bribes to have them released. There must have been many easier ways to make a living. It was difficult, strenuous, time-consuming and uncertain. It required effort and ingenuity which, if applied elsewhere and in another fashion, would surely have brought greater rewards, at least monetarily. But there are people everywhere in the world who prefer the crooked path to the straight, to whom the excitement of dishonesty appeals. It gives them some sense of superiority over the world, a victory over it. It heals or assuages whatever humiliation the world may have inflicted upon them.

'Once it was clear that he wasn't coming back,' said Robert, 'we fell out, my friend and I. Or rather, he fell out with me. He blamed me for what had happened.'

'Why? You were both equally taken in.'

'He became paranoid. He thought I'd set him up with the pastor, that I had been in league with him from the first. He thought I took half the money.'

'Why did he think that?'

'No reason, he just did. Perhaps he was smoking too much dope. He had always been a bit inclined to see enemies everywhere. And my cell is better than his.'

'But surely,' I said, 'he could see that you were still in prison?'

'He thought I was going to be released soon to enjoy the proceeds and leave him alone here. He still believes that.'

'So now he doesn't talk to you?'

Robert laughed a bitter little laugh. 'It's worse than that,' he said. 'He wants to kill me.'

'How do you know?'

'He told me.' He paused. 'Do you know how much it costs to have someone killed here?'

'No,' I replied.

'Ten dollars.'

'Are you saying that he put a contract out on you?'

'Of course he did.' Robert was almost irritated by my slowness on the uptake.

'How do you know?'

'What would you do if you were him and wanted someone

101

dead?'

For Robert it stood to reason, and what stood to reason actually happened. Perhaps it did. No other evidence was necessary.

'He wants to kill me, or rather have me killed. That's why I have to have a bodyguard all the time.'

'And has he a bodyguard too?' I remembered having seen another cell a few yards away with a bodyguard outside.

'Of course. When you want to kill someone, you assume that he wants to kill you as well.'

'And do you?'

'I'll admit I've thought about it. It would be the easiest solution. My life would be a lot better with him out of the way. I could save the money on the bodyguard and use it to get out instead.'

'So could he.'

'It's him who's keeping me in here, not the other way round. I'm his prisoner.'

I looked at my watch. I had sucked the juice out of my visit, as it were, and wanted to go. I invented an excuse.

'I have to meet someone,' I said.

'I'll accompany you to the gate,' said Robert.

My departure from the prison was straightforward. I had clung to my token for dear life throughout my visit, constantly feeling in my pocket to check that it was still there. I had only a small bribe to pay to get my passport back, and it felt more like a tip than a bribe. I had shaken hands with Robert but promised no continued contact, a promise that I knew I should not have kept if I had made it.

As soon as I left the prison, I felt a great weight lifted from me. It had been a matter of only two or three hours, but I had begun already to think I had been in prison for years, so total was the immersion, so enveloping its world.

I returned home. At first I thought of Robert often, but of course with swiftly declining frequency. Was he really under threat or was he imagining it? Was his vigilance prudent or mad? It was impossible to say.

I had all but forgotten him when, three years later, I noticed a very small item in my daily newspaper:

British prisoner murdered in South American Gaol

It was Robert.

The newspaper did not print my photographs. They were too disquieting, the editor said. After all, the newspaper was read round breakfast tables on Sunday mornings.

HOPE

Being entirely ignorant of the science of navigation, even centuries after the voyages of discovery, the aircraft's arrival on the sliver of coral reef in the middle of millions of square miles of featureless ocean seemed to me nothing less than a miracle – a fortunate miracle. How did the pilot find it? But find it he did, and until he did so the presence of a life jacket under the seat meant slightly more to me than it usually did: a ludicrous attempt to calm passengers' anxiety.

As soon as the aircraft door was opened, a blast of hot and humid air entered as if from a furnace, and one realised how puny a thing had been the little cocoon in which we had arrived. Man thinks he is nature's master, when mastery even of his own nature escapes him.

Beyond the coral runway, palm fronds waved in the sea breeze as if in some kind of official welcome arranged by a dictator for another dictator. The airport was really no more than a landing-strip with a small concrete hut for immigration formalities. I was the only passenger, but even my arrival flustered the official because he could not find his rubber stamp among the empty cans of Australian beer that stood on his desk. He was fat, with brown skin glistening with sweat as if he were being basted, a khaki shirt and shorts down past his knees, a canvas belt to keep his stomach in some kind of order, and bare feet with splayed toes toughened by a lifetime of walking barefoot on coral grit. His eyes were bloodshot – he had woken from a beery sleep – but he was friendly.

'Welcome,' he said.

'Thank you.'

As an interim measure before resuming the search for his stamp, he looked at my passport.

'You have come a long way,' he said.

As there was nowhere near from which to have come, this remark was purely formal.

After another search among the cans, he gave up. It was too exhausting, and the whole process was unimportant anyway.

'You can come back tomorrow,' he said. 'I will be less busy.'

It is not only the past that is another country where they do things differently: other countries are other countries too, and not necessarily the worse for that. A disdain for official procedure is attractive – in some circumstances.

The air had been churning with the sound of unseen insects, as if they too had been dragooned into an official welcoming ceremony, but of course I soon learned that it was the invariant accompaniment of daylight in these latitudes. Then I heard the grinding noise of a badly maintained internal combustion engine, mixed with the more grateful sound of a female choir singing happily. A white pick-up truck laden with young maidens in colourful wrap-arounds, with frangipani and hibiscus garlands round their neck and blossoms in their hair (which glistened with coconut oil), drew up and braked so suddenly that it almost pitched them out of the flatbed on which, tightly packed, they stood.

The choir alighted and was led over to me by the driver of the pickup, a man of about fifty in a lava-lava who was accompanied by a woman of stately obesity. Here obesity was dignified rather than slovenly. Perhaps the difference depends on whether being fat is a sign of wealth or poverty.

The man in the lava-lava had the same splayed feet as the immigration officer.

'Welcome,' he said as he approached me, hand outstretched. 'I am Doctor Atonai, Minister of Health. This is my wife.'

'Pleased to meet you.'

One of the young women of the choir stepped forward and draped a garland of sweet-smelling, almost sickly, frangipani round my neck. Apart from bougainvillea, frangipani and hibiscus were the only flowers of the place, but they grew in profusion. Variety is not everything, as those who are accustomed to it think that it is.

I had come to the island on a tour of inspection on behalf of a charity that 'supported' what it called 'health projects' around the world. It suspected that its funds were being improperly employed and had asked for someone who was medically qualified to investigate. It had a duty to its donors, it said, to ensure that their moneys were used to the best effect. Their own largest donor was the government, and I was well-paid.

Its head offices were in London and I was surprised by their comfort, indeed luxury. The charity was called HealthAid (formerly Church Care) and it slogan was *Illness anywhere is illness everywhere*. In the atrium of its office building were pictures of happy smiling lepers and dehydrated babies restored to health. There was a large screen relaying footage of a vaccination campaign in one of the geographically less attractive parts of Africa. The immunised seemed a lot less enthusiastic about it than the immunisers. It was as if the former had been dragooned rather than persuaded, but it was all for their own good. It is difficult to convince anyone of statistical benefits, let alone those for whom official authority and abuse are almost synonymous.

I was interviewed by the trustees and chief executive of the charity. They sat at a long table that made me think of Leonardo's *Last Supper*, in a room (called the Boardroom) that was the latest thing in cool decoration. They were all very earnest, as if any sign of levity or deviation from the utmost gravity would result in someone's death on the other side of the globe. I played the game, for that is what it was.

The chief executive was a woman who dressed like a film star going on an African safari with press photographers in tow. She had to hold herself in readiness to depart at a moment's notice for any tropical country where diarrhoea struck with unusual ferocity. According to the charity's glossy annual report, also peopled by smiling lepers, which I had read while waiting to be called in for my interview, she had last year visited three countries struck by earthquake, one by civil war, four by hurricane, five by flood and three by drought, I presume after their occurrence. It is an ill wind, I thought, that blows nobody any good.

Earnestness is like an epidemic disease: it is catching and it spreads, especially when the earnest are in a position to give or to withhold. In these circumstances, you find yourself uttering platitudes with the conviction of revelation that you would otherwise not permit to escape your lips. You hear yourself talking as if someone else were speaking, which is perhaps not far from the literal truth. Words emerge that you hardly recognise as your own.

'Here at HealthAid,' said the Chief Executive, looking back and forth at the trustees, 'we are passionate about bringing the benefits of modern medicine to the world's poorest and most vulnerable.'

I had come to hate the word *passionate* when pronounced by a functionary. It was indicative of humbug at the service of careerism.

'Commitment is essential,' I said.

She glanced at me as if she would know my innermost thoughts. Was I out-humbugging her, or did I believe it? I think I managed to look innocent. I retained my self-respect by telling myself that I had not said what I was committed to.

'Well,' she said, 'the point is that best practice requires that we ensure that the cycle of value is maintained. You know what the cycle of value is?'

I did. It was a concept recently introduced into hospitals from the supermarkets of three decades ago and taken up with compulsory enthusiasm by hospital managers.

'Yes,' I said, 'set your goals, adopt the method to achieve them, measure your progress towards them, achieve your goals, set new goals. In short, SAMSAS.'

I could tell that she was impressed. I spoke her language: I was the highest type of human, a *team-player* – which was a type rare among doctors.

'You know that we pay only your fare and subsistence?' she

asked. 'Plus a tax free honorarium at the end of your contract.'

'Yes,' I said.

'Then why,' asked one of the trustees, suddenly coming to life like a sleeping adder that had been trodden on, 'do you want the job?'

He was probably a man who had made a fortune and held everyone in either contempt or suspicion who had not tried to do likewise. Trusteeships of charities added to his lustre in his own eyes.

'I want to put something back,' I said, using the debased language of modern philanthropy. I loathed myself for having used it, but the devil drives where needs must, Paris is worth a mass, and so forth. What, after all, is a little cant? If I didn't use it, someone else would.

In short, the job, lasting three months, was mine. I was given a medical – so perfunctory that I could have died the next day, but necessary to avoid the accusation of negligence – and then a ticket. A week later, after a brief explanation of what I was expected to do, I was on the other side of the earth, being driven along a coral track with a truckload of singing maidens behind me.

The local habitations were admirable. They were constructed of coconut logs and matting made of woven pandanus fronds for screens, simple but elegant. These people both had and needed little. Theirs was what an anthropologist had called a generous subsistence. Neither the temperature nor the length of the day varied all year round. Fish, coconut, taro and papaya was their invariant, but complete and sufficient, diet.

How quickly we succumb to the notion and supposed charms of the simple life! Though in the abstract we know that heaven does not exist on earth, we are prepared on the slightest and most superficial acquaintance with a different way of life to ascribe to it a perfection that at the same time we know in our hearts that it cannot have. Ah, we imagine, if only we could live as simply as these people, how happy we should be, instead of which...

It doesn't usually take much time for disillusion to set in, and sometimes for us to go to the other extreme. How terrible it is to live like that, how much better is our own way of life! In the case of the island, it did not take long to discover that life there was far from the trouble-free holiday on a cruise liner of which people dream when they try to think of a perfect existence. Even if a certain Biblical story had not warned us that Man was not made for Paradise (and that, if he were not made for it, the very notion of earthly Paradise for him is incoherent and without content), the inevitable intrusion of the outside world on the island meant that it could not have remained unspoiled, even if it had been perfect to begin with.

But of course, it had never been perfect. When the Europeans came crashing in and established a protectorate over it (from whom? – from other Europeans, naturally), they brought with them such benefits as grog, measles, smallpox, venereal disease and tuberculosis, but they also suppressed the constant fighting with shark-tooth swords and woven pandanus armour that had riven the island since time immemorial. They widened the horizons, which is to say the desires, of the people, and gave a material focus to their discontents. It had never been easy for people to live in harmony on a sliver of land in the immensity of the ocean that doubled in size when the tide went out, so that the relations between them were intense, ritualised and explosive. It must have been like living in a pressure cooker, one that could not always contain the pressure within, and hence the wars that seemed so absurdly Lilliputian to the first European observers. These wars, however drawn out and apparently bitter, resulted in few deaths, for lack of means rather than willingness to kill; and wars that resulted in so few deaths struck the Europeans as primitive in the extreme. Wars in which a third of the population was wiped out would have aroused their respect rather than their derision.

The Europeans brought something more effective than war: alcohol, which acted as a venereal disease of the soul. It was not that alcohol had been unknown before their arrival: the natives or indigenes, as they were then known, knew all about the fermentation of palm-tree juice, indeed they could hardly not have known about it in such climate. But the resultant liquid was weak in alcohol and used only on ceremonial occasions by the older men. The debauchery of the early descriptions was not entirely a figment, but it was caused by those who subsequently described it with such disapproval.

It was not only for the natives that alcohol was a relief, a pastime, a vice and a curse. The expatriate population, small but conspicuous, was likewise given to the bottle. There were a few beachcomber types who had dedicated their lives to the active avoidance of work and who had scoured the world for places where neither labour nor possessions of any kind were necessary. They dealt a little in trade goods to keep body and bottle together, but with the encroachment of the rest of the world on their little paradise they had become the last of their type. The world having grown so small, we shall not look on their like again.

The other expatriates sought tax-free salaries in the sun, or alternatively positions of a degree of responsibility that they would never have had at home. They drank, they said, because there was nothing else for them to do, though it was not always clear what they would have done if alternatives had been available. Their wives had coffee mornings while their house-girls made the bed or swept the verandas of the prefabricated bungalows that went with their jobs, the material legacy of the colonial regime which had ended a decade or two earlier. Next door to my bungalow allocated to me for the duration of my stay lived the general manager of the local radio station and his wife. The radio station was not a slick operation. It would relay the news from Radio Australia through a storm of white noise, though occasionally it would tune in by mistake to Radio Moscow, perhaps the only place in the world where such a mistake could be entirely innocent. As for the local news afterwards, you would hear a rustle of papers in the studio, and then the announcement that 'There is no local news.' Happy the land that has no local news!

The manager's wife was an alcoholic not so much from circumstance as from vocation. Dominating her sitting room was the largest bottle of Scotch I had ever seen, almost as tall as she. It was set on a wrought-iron contraption on wheels, which could be tipped so as to pour out the whisky in large portions. Every lunchtime she would pour herself enough to render her unconscious for the afternoon, and I noticed – not without a certain admiration – how quickly the level of fluid in this gargantuan bottle declined. It was while she was in this stuperose state that a burglar entered the house – one did not lock doors in those days or that place – and stole her engagement ring with a large diamond which she had placed on her bedside table. When he learned of the theft, her husband said, 'I wish he'd left the ring and taken my wife.' His detestation of her was an obsession that added interest to his life; it was almost his hobby.

As soon as I was settled in my temporary home, I began my tour of inspection. HealthAid had sent a couple of million to the island but its representative there, a former nurse, had falsified her medical history and suffered one of her periodic fits of madness, returning to her belief that she was being persecuted by the secret services of the world by means of thought-rays beamed at her from satellites. She had had to be evacuated at great expense, and in addition the charity had to compensate the government of the island for the damage she had done to her bungalow in her efforts to protect herself from the thought-rays. Meanwhile, there had been no control over HealthAid's funds, a replacement for her not having been found because the recruitment process, giving all candidates a fair chance, was so elaborate. It had occurred to the chief executive that the charity's funds might not have been used for their intended purposes, which were the control of tuberculosis, the treatment of leprosy and the rehabilitation of the mad.

It did not take me long to discover that HealthAid's money had brought a lot of benefit, but not to the ill. A new ministry building had been erected to house the extra staff, mostly relatives of the minister, who had been taken on. The minister had a nice new boat, registered in his name, in which he went fishing most afternoons. He said it was necessary to visit the other islands of the archipelago and he also had a splendid all-terrain vehicle apart from the pickup in which he had collected me from the landing strip, explaining to me in the most charming way that all these things were necessary to increase the efficiency of his work. Moreover, he said, he had made no attempt to hide the origin of the funds with which they had been bought. On the contrary, the words 'Purchased with the generous assistance of HealthAid' were prominently displayed on them. How could anyone say, then, that the funds had been misappropriated?

The leprosarium and what was called the Mental Wing were on the periphery of the hospital. They were separated from one another by high wire fences, though who was being protected from whom was not immediately clear. Generally, the lepers seemed to have a higher status than the lunatics: at any rate, they would gather to laugh at them through the fence when they were brought out for their daily exercise under the intermittently watchful eyes of their attendants. Everyone needs someone on whom he can look down or to whom he can feel superior.

Food was brought to both the lepers and the lunatics in large metal pails. It consisted of a pile of taro with a smattering of fish on top. Those who reached the pail first had mainly fish and those who came after had mainly taro. Rudimentary as this diet was, no one starved, and coconuts prevented scurvy.

There was a perpetual physical gloom in the Mental Wing into which the sunlight scarcely penetrated, thanks to the overhanging eaves of the corrugated iron roof. After sunset, it was lit, if at all, by hurricane lamps. Its mephitic smell never left it.

The cells for the patients were small, lined with concrete, and with mean little barred windows just below the eaves. You might have thought it a prison in the Middle East. The beds, so called, were concrete blocks cemented to the wall. In the circumstances, the woven pandanus mat on top of the block, changed but rarely, represented comfort. The inmates were terrible to behold.

There were about thirty of them in all. They had been treated (or incarcerated) for years – incarceration being the greater part of their treatment. As the minister informed me when he accompanied me on my first visit to the establishment, this represented an increase in humanity when compared with the old days – he omitted to say when they were – in which a lunatic would be tied to the trunk of a palm tree and if he failed to recover his sanity in a week he would then be tied to a log and floated out to sea. On a strip of land at most a few hundred yards across, with nowhere else to go, social deviance of whatever type was difficult to tolerate.

The most recalcitrant or dangerous of the patients were chained to the wall: or at least, those reputed to be most recalcitrant or dangerous. In some cases, they had been chained for so long that no one remembered why, the original records having been lost, but since there must have been a reason, and a good one too, it was thought wiser to keep them chained. My suggestion that they should be released was received with horror; in any case, said the Minister, the keys to the padlocks had been lost.

They were like phantoms, these chained lunatics, hollow-eyed and rachitic. My appearance in the Wing aroused no surprise, or any other reaction, in them. They were dead to the world, and the world was dead to them.

Only one of them, Thomas, reacted to my arrival. He gave me a grin that could only be called evil. Thomas was famous, or infamous, on the island: he had cut the throats of his parents for no discernible reason. He had narrowly escaped being lynched, and he might not escape a second time if ever he left the Wing.

There were only four women among the inmates, one of them chained. Their contraceptive was delivered by injection every three months, and their consent was neither sought nor given; they were so distracted that nothing they said made sense and no one bothered with the rigmarole of asking them. The women's section was separated from the men's by a gate of iron bars, through which sexual intercourse between the lunatics took place.

An inmate called Katarina was not able to participate (she still received the injection, however), because she was chained to the wall of her cell. She was notorious, though not for her violence. It was not because she might attack someone, but because she might try to escape, that she was chained. There was also the inertia of past decisions: the continuation of what had been done simply because it *had* been done.

Katarina was clearly mad, as anyone might have been who had been chained for more than ten years with a wall as her main companion. But even now you could see that she must once have been beautiful. She was tall and fine-boned; her face had a natural delicacy that (to my eye at least) was rare among these people, who mostly struck me as coarse-featured. She was a natural aristocrat now in a fallen condition, as after a revolution. The once brightly coloured cloth in which she was wrapped was now both faded and dirty. She was clearly distracted by sound that only she could hear, voices that mocked or menaced her. She responded to them sometimes by laughter, sometimes by anger, and sometimes by a strange combination of the two. The thought that there was no one there who corresponded to the voices never seemed to occur to her, not even after many years. The world had no radius around her, it did not exist beyond her skull; my appearance at her cell door did not register with her in the least. She was now enclosed in a nutshell and counted herself queen of infinite space.

Her hands, with their long, elegant fingers, were in constant sinuous movement, like the antennae of a lobster. These movements were without apparent purpose, driven perhaps by a compulsion without any other possible outlet. They might also have been the consequence of the otherwise ineffective medicine that she was given, also from inertia and just in case she was worse without it.

Katarina's story was told me by a man who called himself *an old hand*, that is to say an expatriate who had lived on the island for much of his adult life. Despite his lengthy residence, however, he had not *gone native*, as the expression had it for those who adopted the way of life and outlook of the people of the island. On the contrary, he remained what he had always been, a scion of the English middle class, whose ambition was to retire to a cottage in the Cotswolds surrounded by hollyhocks. There was nothing dishonourable in this ambition, of course: it was not the kind that would destroy the world, but the effort to achieve it seemed somehow disproportionate to the happiness it would procure. Nothing, however, is disproportionate but thinking makes it so.

His name was Walter Bird, universally known to the other expatriates as Wally. 'Wally by name and wally by nature,' they would say, as if this were a witticism of their own that had never been heard before. Walter himself seemed unaware that he was known by this disrespectful diminutive of his name, and perhaps he really was unaware. He was the highest-ranking civil servant on the island, if that were not too grand a way of describing an administrator in a population that was no larger than that of a smallish municipality. He had arrived young, when the island was still a colony, and being some kind of accountant had gone into the branch of what became, on independence, the Ministry of Finance. He saved most of his tax-free salary for the future cottagey bliss of his retirement.

He was not much liked by the other expatriates, from whom he held himself aloof. He was the largest fish in a small goldfish bowl. This was in the days before computers, but he was said to hold everything about every expatriate in his head. He was believed to be the *éminence grise* of the government, the master of every intrigue real or imagined. I saw no evidence of this. The best plotters are dull, no doubt, but it does not follow from this that the dull are plotters. And Walter was dull.

It was, in a sense, an honour that he should have spoken to me in one of the bars overlooking the turquoise lagoon, with beer served from cool-boxes. Walter was generally an unsocial man who kept himself to himself and was seldom seen outside his office. When not working he was at home with his wife who went about even less than he, and who was thought to be to Walter what Walter was to the other expatriates. He had a small boat in which he went out fishing, but he never took anyone with him. It was far from unknown for people to go missing once their boat had gone over the horizon and was out of view of the island, a fate which some of his detractors wished on Walter: it was he who had the power to grant or withhold their claims to expenses, and it would have taken a more clubbable man than he to have exercised this power and remain popular.

I don't know why he approached me that evening as the sun went down in its usual glorious blaze of colour, so beautiful in the original, so kitsch when reproduced either in photograph or painting. Perhaps he had had a row with his wife that morning and wanted to put off the evil hour – she was something of a tartar at the best of times – of attempted reconciliation. Anyway, he sat down with me having first asked my permission, but without any explanation of his unaccustomed sociability. Perhaps I had been selected for the honour because he knew that I would not be long on the island.

'Do you mind if I join you?'

'Not at all.' In a situation such as mine then was, albeit temporarily, you do not turn down the offer of company.

'My name is Walter Bird,' holding out his hand for me to shake.

I had known who he was but did not say so, in case he thought that others had talked to me about him. He must have known that he was not popular and that anything they said would not have been favourable to him.

I introduced myself by name, not by function.

'I'm the Chief Secretary of Finance,' he said. 'You're from HealthAid, if I'm not mistaken?'

'Seconded by them,' I said, 'on a short-term contract.' I was ashamed of my association with HealthAid, not only because I regarded its money spent on me as wasted but because such wastage was its major activity.

'You're here to find out what has been done with its money?'

'Yes,' I said. 'Its funds must be used in the best possible way,'

'Ah yes, all those charitable old ladies putting their money in the tin.'

'And the government,' I said. 'It makes the largest contribution.'

'They are the greatest experts of all,' he said, 'in wasting money. They waste half of it before they've even collected it. I should know. I am a financial plumber of leaks. As soon as one is repaired, another springs up.'

I took a gulp of my beer.

'And what conclusion have you come to so far?' asked Wally.

'I haven't had time to come to any conclusions. I haven't seen much.'

'Oh, conclusions usually precede the evidence on which they are based,' said Walter, who seemed to be pumping me as Guildenstern pumped Hamlet. 'There is no such thing as an open mind. Minds are either closed or empty.'

Walter had a reputation for knowing everything, at least everything in his little world. He wanted information for filing and future possible use.

'I really haven't come to a conclusion yet,' I said.

'Yes,' replied Walter, 'but if you've been sent all this way to investigate, you must have started out with the idea that there is something to investigate.'

'There always is, as you yourself said.'

'*Touché*,' said Walter, and drank some beer. 'But what have you seen so far?'

'I've been to the Mental Wing. It was horrible. HealthAid sent money to improve it.'

'It's better than it was,' said Walter, 'before the epidemic.'

'What epidemic?'

'The epidemic of cholera. You haven't heard of it?'

I had, vaguely. The epidemic occurred eight years previously, brought by a ship from Peru on which some of the islanders worked as more-or-less indentured labourers. They had come to pick up a load of copra, dried coconut flesh, that was then the main export of the island, for which there was an ever-decreasing demand. Walter's famous and only known *bon mot* was that, since then, the island's main export had been requests for cholera vaccine.

'The Mental Wing used to have twice as many inmates as it has now,' he said. I noted his use of the word *inmate* rather than *patient*. 'It was very overcrowded. The cholera epidemic saw to that. Half of them died, not surprisingly in the circumstances.'

'It could happen again, from what I saw.'

'We'd recognise the nature of the disease sooner. In fact, half of the victims of the epidemic were in the Mental Wing. That was because the sailor who brought it went mad and had to be taken there.'

'The Mental Wing must have been a tremendous incubator for the disease.'

'It was placed under quarantine. Even the lepers next door were evacuated. Raw coconuts were thrown over the fence for food. As it happens, coconut water is a very good treatment for cholera.'

'And the attendants?'

'They fled after the first death. You can't blame them for doing so. Of course, most people thought the Mental Wing had had a spell put on it. That is, in addition to the normal spells that were put on the inmates to send them mad. Even the three local doctors wouldn't enter the Mental Wing during that period because they were afraid of the spell.'

'It would hardly have taken magic to spread cholera there.'

'How else could you explain why the cholera was so severe there, that's what everyone thought.'

'But who put the spell on the Mental Wing and why?'

'There's an inmate there called Katarina...'

'I know, I saw her.'

'Everyone believes she did it.'

'Why?'

'What makes them believe that she did it, or why did she do it?'

'Both.'

'Revenge. They thought she wanted to take her revenge.'

'For what?'

'It's a long story.'

'I have time.'

'Well you see, Katarina was once the great hope of the island. Before I tell you her story, I must tell you something you probably don't know about the island.'

'What, for example?'

'You probably haven't noticed it, but the island's society is completely divided between Catholic and Protestant.'

'What?'

'Yes,' said Walter. 'The wars of religion continue here.'

'Literally?'

'Almost. At any rate, the rivalry is still very strong. Sometimes there are outbreaks of fighting. It is like football back home. They need an outlet for their emotions. It's young men mostly, of course.'

'But fighting over religion?'

'It's a pretext. When the Catholic football team plays the Protestant football team, are they fighting over football or religion?'

'The jealous are not ever jealous for the cause, but they are jealous that they are jealous.'

'Precisely. Young men fight because young men fight. They

need rivalry.'

'But how did it begin, this rivalry of Catholic and Protestant? I mean here, on this island.'

'It began more than a century ago, with the beginning of colonialism. For some reason the colonial powers thought it was strategically important to occupy islands like this. Mainly it was to prevent the others from doing so.'

'There was copra, of course.'

'Hardly the basis of our civilisation. And anyway, they could easily have bought it from the natives if they had really needed it that badly. Some firewater and a few pins would have done the trick. Stone age people are as easy to corrupt as African dictators and much cheaper. No, it was mere school playground bully rivalry that brought the colonists, or rather the imperialists, because they never really colonised the island – here.'

'And that's how the religious rivalry began?'

'In a way. It was the Germans who took some of the islands first but they were not united religiously, of course. They brought their *Kulturkampf* with them.' (Walter was reported by the other expatriates to be a great reader, regarded by them as a type of reproach and implicit criticism. Who did he think he was?) 'They brought Catholic and protestant missionaries with them. For the Catholics the Protestants were heretics, and for the Protestants the Catholics were idol-worshippers.'

'They divided the population?'

'It was already divided between eastern and western half. The two halves used to have their little wars. The Protestants converted the eastern half, and the Catholics the western.'

'And therefore they continued their rivalry?'

'That's putting it mildly. Being so isolated, this island is like an incubator of hatreds. Little things become enormous here. Put two people who mildly dislike each other here, and they soon become murderous. To us these days, because we have no real religious beliefs, doctrinal or theological differences seem trivial and we can't take them seriously, but in the days when the Europeans came, they were still of enormous importance. The islanders took the differences to heart and magnified them to undying hatred. It wasn't enough that they believed that those of the other religion would go to Hell, they wanted to send them there. And of course by then they had machetes and other implements with which to do so.'

'There was a religious war on the island?'

'More than one. It was unfortunate that the first Protestant missionary, Pastor Weissmuller, had been in the army. He taught that the taunts and insults of the Catholics should not go unpunished. He organised his converts into a militia, for self-defence, he said. Father Braun, the first of the Catholics, responded in kind. There was a famous incident in which a convert called Harbo publicly destroyed an image of the Virgin which he said was idolatrous. It was as if the Thirty Years' War had never happened.'

'And the colonial authorities did nothing?'

'Not really. They didn't want the expense of keeping a garrison here; they wanted the colony to pay for itself. They were happy for the missionaries to be the civil authority. Besides, if the Catholics and Protestants were at daggers drawn, the people couldn't revolt against the colony. They were otherwise engaged.'

'But after the Great War, the island became British.'

'Yes, but that didn't change much at first. The German missionaries were allowed to stay, but as they died out, they were replaced by British, Irish and Americans. They stamped out the violence but encouraged the rivalry. Anyway, by then they couldn't have rooted it out, it was too deeply ingrained. It was more peaceful afterwards, however, give or take a riot or two at a sporting contest.'

'And it persists?'

'Oh yes, it is the organising principle of the whole society.'

I brought the conversation back to its starting point.

'That's very interesting,' I said, 'but what has it to do with Katarina in the Mental Wing?'

'Almost everything,' said Walter. He smiled, revealing some yellowing teeth that looked as if they had been filed down to become sharp. 'You see, her father was the first local man to head the local Protestant church. Of course, he still had a missionary adviser or supervisor on hand to keep him on the straight and narrow.'

'The straight and narrow path to where?'

'To victory over the Catholics. But the adviser or supervisor was involved in a scandal and killed himself. It was just as in the story by Somerset Maugham. Do you know it?'

'Yes, very well.'

'Like Davidson in the story, he had an affair. You can't hide anything when you live here. He took an overdose. The missionary society didn't replace him.'

'Why not?'

'Lack of funds, decline in belief in the work, I don't know. Everywhere else with the exception of this island, there has been a rapprochement between the Catholics and Protestants. It had become less urgent, I suppose, to save souls from eternal torment because of idolatry or heresy. Anyway, the failure to replace the supervisor left Katarina's father one of the most important dignitaries on the island. For many, including himself, what he said became the Word of God.'

'What was he like?'

'What was he like? He was dour, rigid, humourless, and bitter.' (That was Walter's reputation too, unfairly I think.) 'If anyone enjoyed something, he forbade it. He was against drinking, singing, and of course fornication. He set up a kind of religious secret police to root out sin.'

'But he had no power to punish.'

'Not legally, but he could excommunicate people by shaming them from the pulpit and preventing them from attending church. It was social death for those to whom it happened.'

'Why?'

'The excommunicants had to leave their families, otherwise he excommunicated the whole family. If you were seen talking to someone who had been excommunicated, you were suspect too. You were given a warning and if there was a second occasion, you were out as well.'

'It was a theocracy, then?'

'If Katarina's father was God, it was a theocracy.'

'Was he... did he keep to his own rules?'

'As far as anyone knows. He never smiled or laughed. He didn't drink or frequent women. He banned the showing of films in the meeting houses from the Protestant half of the island, which was quite an achievement because the people were so fond of them.'

I had gone to a film show on what I now realised must have been the Catholic half of the island. It was held in one of the large thatched meeting houses that every village possessed. A power generator was brought to power the old-fashioned projector and made so much noise that it was difficult to make out the soundtrack above it. Not that this worried anyone; it was the moving pictures everyone had come for. The films were the only window on the rest of the world for those who had never left the island, which was most of them. How peculiar they must have thought the rest of the world! The show I attended was typical, apparently: the films had to be old and at the least third rate to be affordable. First came a long episode of Korean women's wrestling, of whose very existence I had previously had no knowledge, accompanied by the sound of hysterical commentary only just audible over the whirring of the generator, and then a C-category movie (if such a category existed) in which eggs descended on New York from outer space and hatched giant carnivorous lizards that pursued the population as food. After it was over, the army having defeated the lizards but only just, the locals asked me, those who could speak English, whether I had ever encountered any of those lizards, and I suppose that this inability to distinguish between absurd fantasy and reality was understandable in the circumstances. In a world of women's wrestling, why not a plague of carnivorous lizards from outer space? I tried to explain the notion of fiction to them, but we had no language between us of sufficient subtlety for success. I was not absolutely sure that Katarina's father – the Reverend Biribo – was altogether mistaken in his opposition to the showing of films. I thought of them as the fruit of the Tree of Knowledge – if women's wrestling and man-eating lizards counted as knowledge.

'Biribo loved his daughter,' said Walter. 'She was an only child. Her mother died in another childbirth, as did the baby, and Biribo never re-married. He brought Katarina up himself.'

'I suppose this was unusual on the island?'

'Very. Many women died in childbirth, fewer these days of course, but the men usually remarried, to a younger woman. They had more children, too many in my opinion. You've probably noticed the number of children on the island?'

I had. No habitation seemed without a complement of tots with large eyes and protuberant bellies playing around it. They were supposed to be unhealthy according to medical criteria, but they seemed happy enough in their primordial freedom and the boys at least grew up, if the adults were anything to go by, into strapping young men.

'I don't know what's going to happen if the population goes on multiplying like this,' said Walter, suddenly become a modern Malthus. 'It grows by nearly three per cent a year, and they're dependent on outside assistance as it is.'

'Sufficient unto the day is the evil thereof. Something will turn up.'

'Are you Christ or Micawber?' asked Walter.

'Neither,' I replied. 'It's just that projected catastrophes tend not to happen.'

'*Tend* not to happen, perhaps. 'But catastrophes *do* happen.'

'Anyway, the Reverend Biribo and Katarina?'

'Yes, Biribo and Katarina. She was the apple of his eye, of course, but he brought her up very strictly. This was difficult because she was so beautiful. The boys would have flocked around her if he had permitted it. A struggle of wills developed between father and daughter. He wanted her to grow up pure and marry his favourite young pastor who was called Simon. This wasn't what she wanted for herself at all.'

'What *did* she want?'

'It was more what she didn't want, a life with no ordinary enjoyment. The more her father kept her away from enjoyments, the more she wanted them. But she was a clever girl and knew that she had to avoid a direct confrontation with her father that she knew she could never win.'

'What did she do instead, then?'

'She studied hard.'

'That was her way of rebelling?'

'It was what she thought would be her passport to freedom.'

'She would get a job?'

'Oh no, she wasn't thinking as far ahead as that. I doubt that she ever intended to become one of the world's workers. She wanted to go and study in New Zealand and take things from there.'

'Her father allowed it?'

'He objected at first, of course. He had once been to some sort of gathering in New Zealand and regarded the country as a kind of Sodom and Gomorrah. He thought Katarina would be defiled just by touching its soil, let alone by living there.'

'So she wasn't able to go?'

'Under her obedient exterior, she was a high-spirited girl. The island was still a colony in those days, and she enlisted the help of the Governor.'

'How?'

'It wasn't difficult to reach him. It's far more difficult to reach the president now. In fact, he was the last Governor before independence and something of a… a democrat, I suppose you would have to call him. He insisted upon *not* being referred to as His Excellency the Governor. He wore his uniform – you know, tropical whites with a helmet of egret feathers – as rarely as possible. He said it was ridiculous in this day and age, and I daresay he was right. Perhaps it was ridiculous in any age to try to impress people by a mere uniform.'

'I think it appeals to something in human nature.'

'Perhaps. Anyway, the Governor insisted on being called Bill. It was a bit of a joke, 'Bill says this, Bill says that.' He studied hard to speak with a lower-class accent, though he didn't always succeed, because he had been at Winchester. Of course, he was a failure in life, otherwise they wouldn't have sent him here.'

'So Katarina went to see him?'

'Yes. As I was saying, he was some kind of democrat or egalitarian. He believed in every fashionable nostrum, such as women's education, with the fervour of the convert.'

'And so he supported Katarina?'

'Naturally. He believed that countries like this – if you can call it a country – are poor because women were uneducated and underutilised in the work force. That's why it was underdeveloped. Ha!'

'What did he think development of an island like this would consist of?'

'I don't know. Offshore banks, perhaps, some money-laundering. The previous Governor had been in favour of what he called the *Museum Policy*.'

'What was that?'

'He tried to oppose development of any kind and reduced contact with the outside world as much as possible. He didn't like change and said it would only ruin the island. He said it should be kept as an anthropological museum, a kind of living Neolithic exhibit, except that there should be no visitors or as few as possible, and they should be charged a fortune to discourage more of them. They should be allowed to stay only a few days at most.'

'How would the population live?'

'As they had always lived, by fishing and weaving pandanus mats. But it was already too late for that. The worm had entered the bud or, to put it another way, the natives had already eaten of the fruit of the Tree of Knowledge.'

'You mean…?'

'There were things from the outside world that had already become necessities for them, and they wanted more of them. You couldn't shut them off from the rest of the world any more and pretend that it didn't exist.'

'Katarina managed to get the Governor's help?'

'She did. Though he was a democrat, he still had certain powers: quite a few, actually. He more or less blackmailed Biribo.'

'How?'

'Biribo's dream was to build an enormous church, much bigger than the biggest of the Catholics with whom he was in competition. Whoever built the larger church had the deeper faith and truer religion. I suppose it is better than pitched battles, but it was still very wasteful.'

'How did the Governor blackmail Biribo?

'His permission was still needed under a colonial ordinance to build anything above a certain size, and Biribo's proposed church was far larger than that size.'

'So he could have refused his permission?'

'Exactly. And he knew that Biribo had staked his whole reputation on that church. He had promised his congregation that he would defeat the Catholics in the competition.'

'The Governor told him, I suppose, that he could have his

church if he let Katarina study in New Zealand?'

'Precisely. Biribo put it about that the Governor favoured the Catholics in order to foment unrest as a kind of counter-blackmail, but the Governor didn't care. So in the end, all Biribo could do was extract a promise from his daughter that she would behave well in New Zealand.'

'Why was it so important to him?'

'It was a matter of reputation. In a tiny place like this you are judged not only by what you do yourself, but by what members of your family do. There is a kind of collective responsibility. Like father like son, but also like son like father.'

'But if she were in New Zealand, which after all is a long way away, how would he or anyone else know how she were behaving?'

'There were other students from the island there, some of them Catholic. They would be only too delighted to tell tales against her. Besides, he had church connections over there.'

'It sounds as if people here live in fear of others wherever they go.'

'It's inevitable in a small close-knit population. That's what community means.'

'And the loss of community?'

'That's terrible too. You can't have the advantages without the disadvantages.'

'Life is a matter of double-entry bookkeeping, then?'

'There are worse ways of thinking about life.'

It is only in the more out-of-the-way places, in near isolation, that you find philosophical accountants. There is something about isolation that turns a man philosophical, even a man who, if he had followed a more normal path, would never in his life have had an abstruse thought or general idea. If Walter had been, for example, the credit-controller of some large commercial enterprise, he would by this stage of his life have thought of nothing except golf, that sporting metonym for the futility of life.

'If Katarina behaved badly in New Zealand, it would get back to Biribo and the rest of the island,' said Walter. 'And of course it wasn't very difficult to behave badly according to the puritanical standards that Biribo imposed on his congregation. Almost everything that a young person would enjoy was forbidden under Biribo's code.'

'And did she behave badly, or perhaps I should say normally?'

'Of course, and with a vengeance. She was like a dog that had spent all its life on a leash and was suddenly let off in a big wide field. She went wild – according to reports, that is.'

'You didn't believe them?'

'Oh yes, they were perfectly plausible. She took drugs, slept around, went to parties and failed her exams. Her father instructed her to come home.'

'And did she?'

'No. She managed to find a doctor to write a letter and give her a certificate to the effect that she was suffering from chronic fatigue which was why she had not been able to revise for her exams. He said it was the stress of having moved to a totally new environment that had caused it.'

'And did Biribo believe it?'

'No, but the Governor did, and he renewed his threat if he forced her to come home. He said she should be given a second chance. The building of the church was under way by then, but it was always possible to find some regulation that had been violated as an excuse to stop further construction.'

'So the Governor had his way?'

'Oh yes. Like every weak man, he could dig his heels in.'

'Did Katarina behave any better the second time round?'

'A little, or at least she was more discreet. She did more work and passed her exams. But she still went with men.'

'She graduated?'

'Yes, she graduated, and then she came home.'

'What happened then?'

'In those days, to have graduated in New Zealand was still a rare accomplishment for an islander, and so a big welcome home was put on for her. There was a choir at the airport, singing hymns of course, and the Governor turned out for once in his egret feathers because he felt a special pride in the occasion. He was very pleased with himself because it was thanks to him that Katarina had succeeded.'

'And Biribo?'

'By now, he had forgotten all about Katarina's bad behaviour and was basking in the glory which was his too, of course. He forgot that he had tried to prevent her from going to New Zealand. He even claimed that it had been his idea that she should go.'

'But it didn't last, the glory?'

'No. It was still Biribo's wish that Katarina should marry Simon. He was a sleek, oily man, no longer in the first flush of youth, who went round looking for offences to turn the other cheek to and then to praise himself from the pulpit for having done so. There was something insidious about him.' (They said that about Walter too.) 'But there was another reason she couldn't marry him.'

'Which was?'

'She was pregnant. It was from one of her liaisons in New

Zealand.' Walter paused to take a sip of beer: he was a slow, careful drinker. 'At first she denied it, but then it became impossible to deny it any further. Her father insisted that she dress in a Mother Hubbard, which he favoured anyway because it was so unalluring. But she couldn't hide the swelling in her abdomen any longer.'

'What happened then?'

'Biribo was furious, of course. His reputation would be ruined. It was now far too late to send her back to New Zealand for an operation: that's what he would have done if there had been time.'

'He didn't disapprove of abortion, then?'

'He did, for others. But he was thinking of his prestige, not his principles. He wouldn't let her walk about, in case anyone saw the condition she was in. But Katarina knew her father and was very cunning.'

'What did she do?'

'Naturally her father demanded to know who the father of the baby was.'

'Who was it?'

'We still don't have the faintest idea, but she made up a story. She told her father that the father was a New Zealand millionaire called Ross Cambric. She said that she was engaged to him and that he was coming on his yacht to marry her.'

'And Biribo believed her?'

'Yes. You see, she knew her father well. She knew that beneath his veneer of piety there was a deeper layer of avarice. She knew that money would cancel out sin, and more than cancel it out in. She was right. He saw in Ross Cambric an opportunity to make his church so big that the Catholics would have no chance to compete with it. And once it was built, he would lord it over the population. Biribo was ecstatic. He couldn't keep the news to himself and went running to the Governor to tell him, and it soon went round the island. The Catholics were mortified, of course. They thought they had lost the war of the churches.'

'And this Ross Cambric?'

'She made up all kinds of stories about him: how he had made his money, his mansion and farm in the country, his expensive cars, and above all his yacht. It was large, sleek, white and very beautiful.'

'Did everyone believe it?'

'Oh yes, including the Governor. He saw it as a great chance for development, his parting gift to the colony. There were going to be great celebrations to welcome Ross Cambric when he arrived. Nothing like this had ever happened to the island before. The Governor set up a committee in charge of the welcome with himself as chairman.'

'But Ross Cambric didn't arrive?'

'Katarina arranged for someone she knew in New Zealand to send a telegram – there were still telegrams in those days, just – supposedly from him to say that he would be arriving on such and such a date and at such and such a time. The bunting was ready to be hung up, the police band rehearsed – not that rehearsal makes much difference to the way it sounded.'

'And of course Ross Cambric didn't turn up.'

'He couldn't turn up because he didn't exist. But Katarina bought some time with another ruse.'

'Which was?'

'She arranged for a second telegram to arrive to the effect

that he had been taken seriously ill – appendicitis – and had had to be evacuated by helicopter from the yacht on its way here. He would return when he had recovered from the operation.'

'How long did his 'recovery' take?'

'It was very quick because Biribo was growing suspicious and Katarina's pregnancy was advancing. There was a limit to how far the prospect of money could remove the shame of a pregnancy before marriage. She had to be married at least before the baby was born. Fortunately, Ross Cambric was a fit young man and being so rich received the best medical treatment that money could buy.'

'How did he supposedly make his money, by the way?'

'Supermarkets. She even gave the name of the chain, which actually existed. It was just that Ross Cambric didn't own it. But he did promise to open one on the island.'

'Didn't anyone check the story?'

'It wouldn't have been easy from here. Besides, Katarina was very convincing – Biribo now let her out from time to time – and she was so excited by the forthcoming arrival and marriage that everyone believed her. They wanted to believe her anyway, because a yacht had never come to the island before and it would be a great event. Where nothing ever happens, you long for something to happen. It was like a royal wedding in England.'

'And the Governor?'

'He believed in Katarina more strongly than Biribo did. After all, she was in a way his creation and he was her Pygmalion. If it hadn't been for him, she would never have gone to New Zealand in the first place and met Ross Cambric. He didn't want to have to admit that he had been taken in, a gross error of judgement on his part. Governors were supposed to be infallible; that was what they were there for. He might have been a democrat, but he still wanted to be a Pope and he still had his dignity to preserve. And he had been charmed by Katarina, in fact everyone said that he was in love with her. At any rate his wife, known by the expatriates as the Governess, was said to be distinctly unpleased by the interest that he took in her. In fact, someone overheard her referring to Katarina as 'that native slut'.'

'So Katarina arranged for Ross Cambric to arrive again?'

'Yes, in three weeks. The date was set and again the arrangements were made. They were even more elaborate than the first time round.'

'And what happened?'

'The great day came. Ross Cambric had telegraphed his time of arrival. Everyone was out on the shore by the concrete mole that had been constructed years before to receive ships. The Governor was out there in his tropical kit with brass buttons and white feathers. The band was playing, the bunting was fluttering in the breeze. Katarina looked beautiful. Biribo allowed her for the occasion to abandon her Mother Hubbard and wear something more becoming. She looked very alluring with hibiscus in her hair and she was radiant with joy and anticipation. It was her moment of glory. Everyone was straining his eyes, trying to be the first to catch a glimpse of the yacht. It was like trying to hear the first cuckoo of spring.'

'But again he didn't turn up, of course.'

'At the last moment, by which time several people claimed to have spotted a dazzling white ship on the horizon, another telegram arrived. Ross Cambric had died suddenly of a heart attack on board and the yacht had turned back for New

Zealand.'

'Poor man! So young!'

'The crowd was very disappointed, but the Governor was furious. He knew he had been made a fool of, duped, humiliated. His dream of bringing investment to the island had gone up in a puff of smoke, and with it his place in history.'

'How did Katarina react?'

'She broke down in hysterical grief at the loss of her lover and the father of her child, who was now an orphan before he was born. She threw herself to the ground sobbing, and people had to lift her to her feet. She tried to fall again but they propped her up.'

'And Biribo?'

'He was beside himself with rage. He went up to Katarina in public and slapped her in the face. He had to be restrained or he might have done her some real harm.'

'What happened after the crowd dispersed?'

'The Governor said that Katarina must have been mad to have gone from such radiant joy to such hysterical grief, all for someone who might not even have existed.'

'*Might* not have existed?'

'He had to put it like that to make himself look slightly less foolish and gullible than he had been. He had his prestige to maintain. He ordered Katarina to be taken to the Mental Wing.'

'Didn't that make it look as if he had been taken in by a madwoman?'

'He didn't say that she was deluded, he said she was hysterical. It was her emotional state that worried him, he said. Besides, everyone was in the same boat, everyone had been taken in. They all wanted to forget the episode as quickly as possible.'

'And Biribo?'

'He had lost face, of course, but he tried to regain it and was mostly successful. He put it about that Katarina had been Satan's lover in New Zealand who, at the behest of the Catholics, had got her with child. The baby was Satan's.'

'How did that help Biribo?'

'There was a certain glory in having his daughter chosen by Satan. Satan chose her because of his success on the island. Satan was worried that his kingdom was in retreat there. So Biribo said it was more important than ever to build the church as a fortress against Satan's wiles.'

'And people believed him?'

'They said they did and thereby committed themselves to behaving as if they did. Who can tell what people really believe?'

'But where were the funds to build the church to come from?'

'From HealthAid.'

'From HealthAid?' This was unexpected.

'Yes. Its representative on the island was a nurse called Tracy Fuller. She went native, so to speak.'

'What does that mean?'

'She adopted the local ways. She dressed in a Mother Hubbard and lava-lava, put flowers in her hair and began to believe in the same evil spirits as the locals did. She became a follower of Biribo, and some say his lover. She had visions in his church.'

'Biribo must have been pleased.'

'He was no fool, he saw his opportunity. He knew that she was in charge of a lot of funds and that she could be manipulated. People like him can tell the difference between belief and madness. They are better at it than doctors.'

'What did he do?'

'When Katarina was taken off to the Mental Wing, he persuaded Tracy Fuller that it was all Satan's doing and that the way to defeat Satan and make Katarina better was to build the church. It wasn't difficult, she was halfway there already. She transferred all of HealthAid's budget to him.'

'And what about Katarina's baby?'

'It was born one night in the Mental Wing and found the next morning. Katarina had cut its cord with a spoon.'

'And then?'

'The baby was removed from her. Whether it was this that sent her mad or the birth itself, no one knows, but she really did go mad.'

'And never recovered?'

'No, and no one wanted her to recover.'

'Why not?'

''Because all the people still prominent on the island had believed her story of Ross Cambric. They didn't want to be reminded of it. So long as she was confined in the Mental Wing as a madwoman, everyone can forget all about it.'

'And the baby?'

'The baby was taken out to sea one evening after the sun had gone down and was never heard of again. The Governor asked no questions.'